Lincolnshire
COUNTY COUNCIL

COMMUNITIES, CULTURAL SERVICES
and ADULT EDUCATION

This book should be returned on or before
the last date shown below.

31. MAR

05. MAY 11.

01. JUL

24.

D1348102

To renew or order library books please telephone 01522 782010
or visit www.lincolnshire.gov.uk
You will require a Personal Identification Number.
Ask any member of staff for this.

EC. 199 (LIBS): RS/L5/19

LARGE PRINT   £6.50

L 5/9

THE SPY IN PETTICOATS

For the sake of her country Letty had agreed to undertake a dangerous mission playing the part of her brother Greville — it was madness. She had accepted the assistance of the naval architect David Gray, a man she had grown to love. What would she do when she had to don her ruffles and petticoats once more and leave Mr. Gray? Before their agonising farewell, fate placed them both in a perilous position, and they had to make their way into enemy France to escape safely once their mission was over.

Books by Katrina Wright
in the Linford Romance Library:

KATRINA WRIGHT

THE SPY IN PETTICOATS.

Complete and Unabridged

LINFORD
Leicester

First published in Great Britain in 1984

First Linford Edition
published February 1993

British Library CIP Data

Wright, Katrina
  The spy in petticoats.—Large print ed.—
Linford romance library
I. Title II. Series
823.914 [F]

ISBN 0–7089–7328–0

Published by
F. A. Thorpe (Publishing) Ltd.
Anstey, Leicestershire

Set by Words & Graphics Ltd.
Anstey, Leicestershire
Printed and bound in Great Britain by
T. J. Press (Padstow) Ltd., Padstow, Cornwall

1

"BUT Greville," Letty said for the ninth time, her delicate forehead wrinkling with perplexity, "I can quite understand that you should be ordered to the Admiralty, after all, you are a commander in the Navy. But why is it so imperative that I come with you? The Admiralty cannot possibly be interested in me."

Her brother leaned across in the swaying coach, which had been sent to fetch them from the family home in Kent, and patted her gloved hand.

"Dear sister, I have told you that I don't know. No doubt all will be revealed when we reach London."

London! In spite of herself, Letty could not help a flurry of excitement, for in her twenty-three years, she had never visited the metropolis before; her eccentric Papa seemingly having forgotten that he possessed a daughter as well as a son, and having made no provision for her to have any social life whatsoever, beyond the country pleasures on the estate and in the nearby villages. And since Letty was Miss Letitia Fanshawe, 'the Young Lady from the Big House', it had not been seemly for her to indulge in the sort of horse-play a country wench was allowed.

Her Papa had remembered to hire first a governess, and later, a companion, for her, but for the rest, he spent his days largely patrolling the battlemented roof of Greville House, Greville being a family name, with a telescope, keeping watch on the distant glitter that proclaimed the existence of the sea, and preparing to defend his estate should the villianous Napoleon, or any other foreign foe, invade England.

In their childhood years, Letty and Greville had become very close, firstly, since they were twins, which gave them one bond of affection, and also since their mama had died at their birth, leaving them to the care of a well-meaning, but somewhat slovenly Nanny; a nursemaid who drank in secret.

Later, when they grew older, Papa had proudly watched his son depart to become Midshipman Fanshawe of His Britannic Majesty's Navy, and fight the 'foreign foes' he had always feared might attack Greville House. And while her brother was experiencing a wide and exciting life on the high seas, rising rapidly to his present rank of commander, Letty, forgotten by her father, spent her days desultorily wandering in the parkland, practising her singing, and stitching endless embroidery in the short-sighted company of her companion, Miss Drew.

Greville's occasional visits were the only lively spots in her existence.

On this occasion, he had hardly arrived home when he had received a summons from the Admiralty for both himself and 'your esteemed sister, Miss Letitia Fanshawe' to go to London at once, 'on important business.'

"Whatever can it be?" Letty asked, when the message arrived, and a coach from the Admiralty stood waiting while they packed, for they had been warned that they might have to stay for some time.

"I don't like it, Miss Letty, I really don't," Miss Drew declared emphatically, blinking behind her round spectacles. "Why should you have to go to that wicked city, and what important business could the Navy possibly have with you?"

"It says we must be very discreet," Letty warned her, looking round cautiously. "Don't speak about this to anyone after I've gone, will you, Miss Drew?"

"Indeed I won't. But what does your father say about it?" Miss Drew asked, and the young woman shrugged.

"Grevile just told him we were going to London for a while. He didn't seem

4

to mind. You know he takes no notice of my presence. He will not even realise that I have gone."

"But London! Oh, I do hope you will be safe, Miss Letty," Miss Drew said, clasping her hands anxiously.

Letty replied rather sharply, "I shall be accompanied by my brother. Kindly remember that. Anyway, it is high time I saw something of the world. I should die of boredom if I thought I was never to leave this house for the rest of my life."

The maid appeared to announce that her box was ready, and Greville came striding into the morning-room, where she and Miss Drew were sitting. Letty went up to her room to collect her reticule, her gloves and cloak, and to check that the maid had not forgotten to pack anything she might require, then she took a last look round. Her eyes were sparkling, and her cheeks were flushed. What excitement awaited her before she saw this room again? Life was beginning for her at long last.

"And about time, too," she said to herself, as she put her cloak round her shoulders, and lifted her bonnet to her piled-up flaxen hair, before going to join Greville in the coach.

★ ★ ★

They rumbled towards London, and Letty leaned out of the coach window, her spirits high, as the unfamiliar scenery passed by. Greville sat opposite her, looking magnificent, she thought, in his uniform.

"Oh, how exciting this all is," Letty said. "Do you know, Greville, for the first time in my whole life, I feel as if I am really alive. I felt entombed in that house with each day as boring as the next."

"But surely you were occupied with running the household, and that sort of thing?" her brother said.

Letty shrugged. "Mrs Tempest is the most efficient housekeeper that ever was. I spent most of my time with

Miss Drew, and she's enough to drive anyone to distraction."

"Poor darling? Didn't you have any gentlemen callers?" Greville asked, with interest. "You're a beauty, you know, Letty, especially this morning, with your bright eyes and pink cheeks. I should have thought there would have been a wedding long ago."

"Oh, it's obvious you don't know the first thing about my way of life," Letty declared. "I had two beaux."

Greville started to say, "Well, then — " but his sister cut him short.

"One was sixty if he was a day — it was our neighbour, Mr Hallam, who has been a widower for the last few years. The other was another local gentleman, Sir Oliver Rivers, who is thirty-five, tall, dark and handsome."

"And what was wrong with him?" Greville asked.

Letty gave him a sharp glance. "Oh, nothing. Except that almost all the babies born in the village bear a remarkable resemblance to Sir Oliver. And that he has gambled away his father's fortune and only wished to marry me for mine, so that he could continue living in the style to which he is accustomed. His very eyes made me shiver. He is as cold as an icicle. No, Greville, I'm afraid there were not many eligible husbands to choose from. But I always thought something would happen one day — and now this. Why do you think I have been summoned to the Admiralty? What can they possibly want with me?"

"I am as much in the dark as you," Greville told her.

Nevertheless, she continued to speculate all the way to London, until at last, as evening was drawing in, they reached the outskirts of the City, and Letty's attention was fully occupied by the sights and sounds they passed as the coach made its way to a comfortable-looking hostelry. The driver informed them they were to spend the night there and they would be taken to the

Admiralty in the morning.

Every provision had been made for their comfort, and after an excellent meal, Letty, who was tired with all the excitement, retired to the small, but clean pleasant room that had been reserved for her. She slept like a child, and awoke to hear the sounds of the street vendors and the great heart of London throbbing to the start of a fresh, new day.

★ ★ ★

Inside the imposing halls of the Admiralty, next morning, Letty waited with Greville, her heart beating fast with excitement, while figures hurried to and fro. A menial came towards them, a sheaf of papers in his hand.

"Commander Fanshawe? Will you be so good as to come this way, please?"

Greville rose, and Letty rose also to accompany him, but the menial held up a restraining hand.

"Miss Fanshawe, I should be obliged

if you would remain here for the moment. Each of you will be interviewed separately."

Bewilderedly, Letty sat down once more, while, with a raised eyebrow cast in her direction, Greville disappeared down a passage. In a few moments, the menial was back, and he bowed to her deferentially.

"I regret the delay, Miss Fanshawe. If you would now accompany me?"

She was led off in a different direction, and the menial knocked discreetly at a heavy door. A voice within bade him enter, and he opened the door and stood aside.

"Miss Letitia Fanshawe, sir," he intoned, as Letty swept into the room, where a figure in uniform was seated at a large desk. He rose to greet her.

"Miss Fanshawe." He came round the desk and bowed over her hand. "How good of you to come. Pray be seated." And he indicated a comfortable chair, a little to one side of the desk. Letty gathered her skirts and sat down with as much composure as she could. She looked up at her host expectantly.

"No doubt you are wondering why we have summoned you here," the man said, with a smile that transformed his stern face, and she nodded. He began to pace the room, his hands clasped behind his back.

"Well, where shall I begin? First of all I have some questions to ask you." He looked sharply at her. "Do you love your country, Miss Fanshawe? Are you a young lady of courage and integrity? Can you keep your own counsel?"

Letty did not quite know what to answer. "Yes, sir, I love my country," she said slowly. "And I believe I can keep my own counsel. As to my courage and integrity — they have never been tested. But I hope I would be able to carry through any undertaking to which I pledged myself."

He was regarding her quizzically.

"I will be frank with you, Miss Fanshawe. Your brother, Commander

Greville Fanshawe, we know to be a man of outstanding bravery, resolution, and quick wits. We hoped that his sister would prove to possess these same qualities, for there is a task to be done. And only you, of all the people in England, can do it."

"Me, sir?" Letty echoed, completely bewildered.

"Yes, because you and your brother are twins, and are very similar in appearance," was the amazing answer. "You see, Miss Fanshawe — and what I am about to reveal to you must not be repeated to anyone outside this room — we need someone to impersonate your brother. For a few days only, you understand. And because of your likeness to him, you are the only one we can call upon. You would require to be dressed as a man, in a uniform like your brother's and to assume his name and rank. Your hair would have to be dressed as much like his own as possible. And to all intents and purposes, for the vital week, you would be your brother, Commander Greville Fanshawe."

Letty sat with wide eyes and stared in disbelief.

The man smiled sympathetically. "I have startled you, but that was only to be expected," he apologised. "You think I am mad, perhaps, Miss Fanshawe? Well, these are times that call for mad plans, dangerous plans, and people who are willing to undertake them."

Letty's brain was very quick. "I understand what you have said, sir," she replied, after some moments. "But while I'm impersonating Greville, if I agree to this rather fantastic scheme, what will he be doing? And why not beneath his own name?"

"Ah! Now we come to the nub of the matter," the man said, giving her an approving glance. "You are shrewd, ma'am. Your brother had been chosen for a highly dangerous, secret mission. He must penetrate the very heart of the French Admiralty in Paris and gain certain information we require. He must, therefore, travel quickly, and in disguise. And, once having obtained the facts we need to know, he must leave France by the most speedy method possible, assuming his own personality as soon as he can, in order that he will not have been missed. But — " he lifted a finger, "during the days while he is in France, he must appear to be seen going about his duties because French spies are everywhere. And that, Miss Fanshawe, is where you come in. For you will take his place, so that nobody, not even his own associates, will know, or even suspect, that he is anywhere else but where you are."

"And where will I be?" Letty asked calmly.

"You will be leaving England to join Rear-Admiral Sir Charles Duncan's flag-ship," he informed her. "The rear-Admiral's squadron is at present blockading Brest, where part of the French fleet is anchored, and his Lieutenant has been summoned to

England on official business. He knows nothing of the real reason why we have called him home, But it is so that Commander Fanshawe can sail out abroad the frigate which brought him here to take his place temporarily" He paused, then added, "Commander Fanshawe, of course, will be none other than yourself."

Letty drew in her breath, and her hands tightened on her reticule.

"But, sir," she began, and stopped with a shrug.

He prompted her, "Yes, Miss Fanshawe?"

"Even if I were to agree to impersonate Greville — which, should it protect him in a dangerous undertaking, I shall do — how could you ever imagine I could get away with the impersonation? I know nothing about ships, I have never been close to the sea. I would not know what to do nor what to say. Letty told him.

The man in uniform nodded agreement.

15

"We had taken that into account, of course. You will not be expected to do anything except appear in the person of your brother, so that the men can see you. And in order to protect you from too close contact with any sailor, or to advise you should things become difficult, you will have a mentor with you who will do his best to make certain that the impersonation passes off successfully. As I told you, it will be for only a few days."

"Mentor, sir?" she seized on the word hopefully.

"We are sending Mr David Gray, a naval architect, to Brest with you," he explained. "It will be under the pretext that he has to make a report on the Rear-Admiral's ships. He is waiting in the next room. One moment."

He went to an inner door, opened it, and spoke briefly to someone out of Letty's line of vision. A man walked in, and as she looked at him, and he smiled at her, Letty felt the blood rise in her cheeks, while her heart suddenly began to pound very fast, and her knees went weak.

The older man was introducing Mr Gray to her, but his voice came to Letty through a roaring in her ears, and all she was conscious of was the tall, muscular figure in the blue coat, with a floral waistcoat, and white lace at throat and wrists. And when Mr Gray bent over her hand, and his lips touched her glove, she felt as though the formal kiss had burned through to tingle on her skin, and was so magnetised by his handsome face, with its fair hair and steady gray-green eyes, that she could hardly manage to reply.

"How do you do, Mr Gray?" she said, unsteadily.

A week of proximity with this man! Would she be able to stand it? But even more important, would she be able to stand it when they had to part? For Letty saw before her all the dreams she had ever dreamed about in a man, come to life, and she knew that

17

now that she had met him, she never wanted to leave him again.

She tried to pull herself together and behave normally as Mr Gray lounged against the side of the mantelpiece and the older man continued to speak to her.

"Mr Gray will be sailing with you to Brest, as I said, and for the few days when you will be required to impersonate your brother on the flagship, he will be constantly at your side to give you all the assistance he can. The rear-Admiral is aware of the plot, but no one else aboard has any idea of it. You are a brave young woman, Miss Fanshawe, as well as a beautiful one, and I have every confidence in you."

Letty tried to speak calmly. "You say the impersonation will be for only a few days, sir. What is to happen then?"

"Ah, yes. Well, I have told you that your brother, who is even now being briefed in his mission elsewhere, will need to escape from France," the older man said, as he paced the room once more. "He will make his way, in disguise, of course, to Brest. There, he will be picked up under cover of darkness and brought to the flag-ship. He will then resume his own clothes, his own identity, and your part will be over. All aboard the ship will be able to swear that he has been with them ever since the frigate brought him from England."

"And what will happen to me?" Letty queried. "I cannot very well suddenly appear from nowhere."

"I am afraid you will have to undertake a second role," said the officer, and smiled. "You will be discovered as an English lady in distress, who is trying to escape from France to join her family in England, and your appearance on board the ship will be engineered so that the men will see a lady, in tattered clothing and unkempt state, being rowed from the land to safety on the vessel.

"Your situation will be explained to them — you can choose any suitable name you wish as an alias — and you will of course disappear into private quarters, until the rear-Admiral despatches you, together with Mr Gray, in a frigate back home. For the sake of appearances, Commander Fanshaw will remain on board for a few more weeks, until we can replace him with the real Lieutenant. His information from the French Admiralty, which we need so badly, will be smuggled back by Mr Gray. I think that explains everything."

"Yes, indeed," Letty said, marvelling at the way in which every problem had been anticipated and overcome. "But do you think I am capable of carrying out what you require of me? If it will help Greville, I will willingly do my best, but if something should go wrong . . ."

"That is why I will be with you, Miss Fanshawe," David Gray reassured her. "You will not be alone. I promise you, if you have the courage to undertake this mission, I will see to it that no harm comes to you. Nor, if I can prevent it, to your brother. I will do everything possible to make things easy for you. Will you trust me?"

She looked up blushingly, into his face, and, involuntarily, her answer came. "Yes. Oh, yes."

"Then that is settled," the older man said briskly. "I will see whether your brother's briefing is complete, Miss Fanshawe, and tomorrow, the enterprise begins. You will be visited by various people at your hostelry, who will disguise you as Commander Fanshawe. Then, tomorrow afternoon, Mr Gray will arrive to take you on the first stage of your journey, while your brother sets out in secret. And, Miss Fanshawe — He paused, then added gravely, "You will be doing your country inestimable service. I thank you, on behalf of all who are concerned with the safety of England, from the bottom of my heart."

* * *

Once Letty and Greville were reunited, and on their way back to the hostelry in a coach, Greville seized Letty's hand, his face set grimly.

"What did you say to this preposterous scheme, Letty? I must do my duty and go on my mission, but the thought of you involving yourself in such machinations . . . "

"I agreed to impersonate you, of course," Letty said calmly. She smiled. "It will be quite diverting."

"I'm worried about your safety. It could be dangerous, you know, should anyone suspect, Greville fretted.

Letty looked down demurely. "I am certain that I shall be quite safe. There is a — a Mr Gray coming with me, who is going to make sure that everything runs smoothly. He's a naval architect," she said, going on to tell her brother all about him.

Greville had relaxed during her explanation, and the corners of his mouth rose in a grin.

"He is exactly the man you have dreamed of all your life. I begin to see why you are so anxious to put yourself in my place. Romance is written, as plainly as can be, all over your pink cheeks and shining eyes. Mr Gray, eh? And you think he will look after you?"

Letty raised a radiant gaze to her brother. "Oh, Greville, I would place my life in his hands. He is so tall and handsome and — and I feel that he will protect me from any danger, that he is like a rock. I cannot help myself. I love him."

"Well, I wish you luck," Greville said, more soberly. "I know you are brave and spirited, darling sister, and if this venture brings you the man of your dreams, no one will be more delighted than I."

"Your part is the dangerous one," Letty pointed out, and he shrugged.

"It will all be over soon, and we will be together again. Danger is something

I live with constantly, Letty." He gave her a quizzical glance. "It will be interesting to see how you look when you have been transformed into myself."

2

THE following morning, discreet visitors made their appearance at the hostelry, and Letty was fitted out with a man's attire; the blue coat, white breeches, trappings of authority that made up the appropriate uniform.

A small man cut away her flaxen hair until it was the right length to be worn, as a gentleman would wear his shorter locks, in a queue, tied with a ribbon.

"Very tidy, miss, very tidy indeed," the man said, as he sprinkled her hair with powder. He stepped back to admire his handiwork. "A right, fine, upstanding, young gentleman you look, if I may say so. Just the final touch — your hat."

A tricorne was placed carefully upon Letty's smooth head, and carefully adjusted to the right angle. Another servant stepped forward with a sword, which was strapped round Letty's slender waist, and when she moved towards the mirror, feeling most unusual in the polished boots that had replaced her usual, dainty slippers, the scabbard of the sword slapped smartly against her side.

To her incredulous gaze, the figure of her brother stared out at her; a little slighter, perhaps, than the real Greville, but when she straightened her back in military fashion, and pulled her shoulders straight, she was certain that anyone who did not know Greville would be deceived into thinking that she was her brother.

"It's uncanny," she declared, and the gentleman who had been in charge of her changed appearance rubbed his hands in a satisfied manner.

"I can see that the undertaking will be an immense success — an immense success," he repeated emphatically. As she turned from the mirror, he continued, "Your brother's sea-chest will make up your luggage. He will require it himself when he resumes his own identity. Suitable attire for you, once you must return to femininity again, will be secretly packed and transported to the Rear Admiral's flagship. Now you have half an hour to say farewell to the Commander, before he sets out on his mission. And, from the moment he leaves this hostelry, you will be Commander Greville Fanshawe. Do not forget it, even for a moment, or you may place yourself and your brother in deadly peril. Because, as you know, French spies are everywhere.

"I will take my leave of you, with your permission, and wish you well in your enterprise. Mr Gray will be here early this afternoon and, from then on, you will be his responsibility." He bent over her slender hand, which felt curiously naked without her gloves, and then he and his men left, leaving Letty still bemused by her transformation.

The door opened, and a man that Letty did not recognise came in, saying hastily, as she drew herself up and frowned, "It's me. Your brother. What do you think of my disguise, eh?"

A tattered coat and breeches, fair hair skilfully made to appear unkempt and grubby, down-at-heel boots, and hands and face miraculously those of a weathered labourer, not an officer of His Majesty's Navy, had completely altered Greville's appearance.

Letty gasped. "Greville" Why, I would never have recognised you in a hundred years!"

The weathered face grinned at her, revealing a flash of white teeth.

"Well, speaking for myself, I would certainly have recognised you, Commander Fanshawe. What miracle has turned my little sister into me? I could swear I was looking at my own reflection. Letty, I do believe you will carry it off!"

"I'll try not to disgrace your name, Greville," Letty said, a little tearful now that the moment of parting had come. She embraced her brother fondly. "Do be careful, won't you? I don't know quite what you have to do, but please, please come back safely."

"Don't worry, little sister, I will," he reassured her. "We'll soon be together again aboard the Columbella. I'll take every care, I promise you. And you too, God keep you safe, until we meet again."

"How Miss Drew would swoon if she could see me now, and knew the part I have to play," Letty said, trying to be cheerful.

Greville added, "It's fortunate I told Papa we might be in London for some time. Little did I realise that such an adventure awaited us, when we set out from home. But don't worry, Papa need never know anything, and I doubt whether he would take much notice even if we were to tell him. Now then, I must be off. When is your beau coming to collect you?"

In spite of herself, Letty flushed. She had told Greville how she thought herself to be in love with Mr Gray.

"He is not my beau, Greville. Why, I have set eyes on him only once, for a few moments."

"But those few moments were enough!" her brother declared, gaily, and Letty gave a reluctant smile.

"He's coming early this afternoon. Oh, Greville, do you think he could possibly ever come to love me? I mean, all the time I am with him, I shall look like a man."

"He won't think of you as a man," her twin promised her. "He'll think of you as he saw you yesterday, in that pretty, green, muslin gown. And if he has any worth, he will love you for your spirit, your courage and your integrity — for you have all these, little sister."

He took her hands, and gave her a farewell kiss on the forehead. "Good-bye now, Letty. Take good care of yourself."

"You too, dear Greville," Letty said emphatically.

A few moments later, she was alone.

★ ★ ★

At first, when David Gray came to collect her from the hostelry, Letty had been awkward in her naval clothes, half-defiant, half-shy, because she was so afraid he might not think well of her. But as they settled into the coach that was to transport them to the docks of Portsmouth, and the frigate that awaited them, he semed to sense her shyness, and did his utmost to put her at her ease.

"The resemblance to your brother is remarkable, my dear Miss Fanshawe," he commented, smiling at her with warmth in his grey-green eyes. "But I cannot help thinking of you as you sat in that room in the Admiralty, and the dainty gown you wore, with all the trappings of femininity, the bonnet and parasol and gloves. You were like some sweet nymph of the woodland, bringing the scent of lilies-of-the-valley into those fusty rooms."

Letty blushed. "I hope no one will

guess that I am not a man," she ventured hesitantly, her heart beating fast at his words. "For then I would be putting Greville's life in danger."

"Rest assured, no one will guess. It is a secret between the two of us," he told her confidently. "And since we are to be spending at least a week together, can we not dispense with the formalities? Or would you be offended if I were to ask you to address me as 'David'?"

"Oh, no, indeed not," Letty replied quickly, a blush mounting in her cheeks once more. "But if I am to call you David, then you must call me — why, what must you call me? If you were to address me as 'Letty', it would give away the fact that I am not a man." Her face fell. "I suppose you will have to call me 'Commander', or something similar."

"I meant, when we were alone and in private," he said gently. "Naturally, we will be extremely formal on any occasion when we might be overheard.

But when we are alone, and can relax our vigilance, shall we agree to be David and Letty to each other?"

Letty bowed her pink cheeks and murmured, "That would please me very much."

"So! We are going to be friends, then," David declared cheerfully. "And I must tell you, Letty, that I admire and respect your courage in undertaking this venture. If you have any problems, or are in any difficulty, come to me at once. Now, I think it would do no harm if I were to prepare you for some of the things you will see and the terms you will hear used at sea."

And for the next hour or so, while Letty listened intently, he explained a little of what she might expect to find as she played her part. She tried to remember everything, for even the tiniest slip could mean danger for Greville.

* * *

At Portsmouth, with the bustle of the docks surrounding them, David steered Letty through the crowds, and then murmured, "Ah, there we are. A boat is waiting to row us out to the frigate. Try to behave as I have instructed you, and all will be well."

Sailors loading and unloading cargoes, women with brazen faces, officers stalking like gods among lesser beings, all receded as Letty looked out to the forest of masts and spars that crowded the harbour, with the glittering sea beyond. Her heart beat fast, for there was something exciting and thrilling about the scene, like a painting come to movement and life. She thought she undertsood, then, a little of what fascinated Greville so much about the career he had chosen.

For herself, she was on edge with tension, but not afraid. Those grey-green eyes and the pleasant, deep voice of the man beside her had given her confidence.

She walked among the hustling

sailors, hearing the strange noises of the waterfront, as she imagined her brother would have walked, head high, hand carelessly on his sword-hilt.

She was careful to show no untoward feelings of hesitation or strangeness as she stepped into the boat that was to transport herself and David Gray to the frigate. She had been rather apprehensive that she might disgrace herself and destroy their carefully laid plans by being sea-sick, however, once the ship finally set sail, she found the motion pleasing, not the slightest jot unsettling to her stomach.

What did cause her a certain amount of embarrassment, though, was the fact that she and David Gray were to share a cabin. Although there were two bunks, she could just imagine what Miss Drew and all the other ladies of her acquaintance would think, not to mention the sly glances and digs in the ribs in which the gentlemen would indulge, if they were to be told that she had slept, confined in a small cabin, alone with a man!

Not that she herself had any fear of him. They were comrades in arms, and as soon as he decently could, once the door was firmly shut behind him, and she was obviously letting her dismay reveal itself upon her face, he took the small step towards her that was all the distance the cabin afforded, and grasped her by the shoulders, looking her squarely in the eyes.

"Letty, this was the only way. Captain Swallow is not aware of the plan, and the Admiralty had to make up some story about my requiring to consult you on certain matters, so that we would need a separate cabin in which to work. You could not have bedded down in a hammock with the midshipmen in the orlop, or even, to be more precise, with the other Lieutenants of this vessel in the officers' mess."

Letty made a motion of her hand to sweep back her hair, forgetting that she now wore it in a man's queue, at the nape of her neck.

"It was just that I had not expected — " she faltered, and summoned up a smile that made her eyes flash with mischief. "After all, I am compromising you, just as much as you are compromising me," she declared gaily. "What will your prospective wife — if you have one — say to that?"

"I have no prospective wife," he said, with unexpected seriousness, then gave here a long look and added significantly, "yet."

Letty felt happiness bubble up in her heart. He was not promised — but there had been a promise for her in his last word. She felt like throwing her arms round his neck, but restrained herself, and instead, asked as calmly as she could, "how will we manage?"

"We will," he assured her, and pointed out with a flash of gaiety in his own voice, "Don't forget now, you are a man, you have a nightshirt packed in your chest, and not a lady's frills and fripperies. I can always turn my back or stand outside the door while you don your nightshirt."

"Then I will have to turn my back while you don yours," she said daringly, and he laughed.

"Any other young lady would swoon, but you have spirit, Letty. I can see that you will make an excellent Commander Fanshawe."

"All the same," Letty said, her face averted. "I am glad you saw me in a gown, with all my 'frills and fripperies', before you met me dressed as a man."

"My first sight of you is something I shall never forget," David told her, and took her hand gently. "Letty, when all this is over — "

He was interrupted by a knock upon the door, and instantly, the two of them had the width of the cabin between them. David muttered, "Damn!" as he opened the door, and was informed that the Captain requested their presence at his table at dinner that evening. He replied, as graciously as he could, and shut the door again. When he turned back to Letty, his face was set in grim lines.

He sighed. "This is no time to speak of personal matters. We must not forget that we have a mission to carry out. Our feelings must wait. I think it would be wise if we were to take a short walk on deck and show ourselves. We cannot spend all our time together in the cabin, and we must not forget that though we have seeming privacy, we maybe overheard even here."

"Yes, you are right," Letty said calmly. But her heart was singing. If he had been about to say what she thought he had, it meant that he probably loved her too. And, after their mission was over, perhaps he would declare himself, and she would never have to leave him. Until then, though, they must not forget the danger both to the two of them and to Greville . . .

So with her inner happiness keeping her spirits high, Letty enjoyed the voyage to Brest. She loved to feel the motion of the deck beneath her feet, and the wind tugging at her bound-back hair. She developed a swagger to go with her masculine attire, and David told her, with an approving smile, that she was carrying off her part perfectly.

It was only during the first night at sea that she woke after drifting into an uneasy sleep, in the grip of a terrible nightmare where she saw Greville held by soldiers, blood running down his face, and was unable to hold back her sobs. In the darkness, David lit a lantern, and came to where she sat huddled in the unfamiliar nightshirt, a bundle of misery, tears streaming down her face.

Gently he put an arm round her. "What is it, Letty? Are you afraid?"

She managed to shake her head and still her sobs a little. "No — no. I dreamed I saw Greville being beaten up by soldiers. Oh, I do hope he is safe!"

"He will be," David told her comfortingly. "He's brave and gallant, and very quick-witted. He will be able to extricate himself from any awkward situation in which he finds himself, don't fret."

"It was so real," Letty moaned, and he pulled her against his shoulder.

"There! Cry if you want to. It was only a nightmare."

The touch of his arms and his strong shoulder was infinitely comforting, and Letty soon pulled herself together.

"You must think I am very silly, to be frightened so by a nightmare," she said.

He replied soothingly, "Not at all. You are my brave girl, and what you're doing would be a strain for anyone. But don't fear. You'll see Greville soon." His hand stroked her hair, loose round her shoulders, now.

After a few moments more, he let her go, and she sighed and lay down once again.

"I shall have to put out the light,

or someone may see it and imagine something is amiss," David told her.

She nodded sleepily on her pillow. "I shall be all right now."

He extinguished the lantern, and she heard him return in the darkness to his own cot. How comforting it was to have him so near. She fell asleep again, and this time, slept the sleep of exhaustion until his hands gently shook her and told her it was time to rise.

3

OUTSIDE the harbour at Brest, a magnificent sight met Letty's eyes. The English ships of the Rear-Admiral's squadron were patrolling the entrance, and she could see some of the masts of the French vessels cooped up inside the harbour, their spars vivid against the blue sky.

She and David bade farewell to Captain Swallow, and descended the ladder to the boat that was waiting to row them across to the Rear-Admiral's flagship, which gleamed and glittered in the sun with its gilding and scroll-work. Once aboard, they were received by the Rear-Admiral himself, who conducted them to his cabin, with orders that he was not to be disturbed.

The cabin, magnificently furnished, made Letty catch her breath as she looked round in wonder.

The Rear-Admiral smiled kindly at her. "Is this what you expected on a rough ship, Miss Fanshawe?" he asked, and at the sound of her real name, her head reeled. For a moment, she had forgotten that Rear-Admiral Sir Charles Duncan was aware of the plot, and her deception.

"Oh, sir, you gave me the fright of my life," she admitted, breathlessly. "I am so used to being addressed now as Commander Fanshawe, and treated as a man. For a moment, I thought someone had found me out, I had forgotten you know that I'm not really my brother."

"You make a fine, up standing officer and gentleman, ma'am," Sir Charles told her. Then added, "However, in the future, I think it would be wisest if I were to continue the deception and address you as though you were indeed the replacement for my First Lieutenant, which you are intended to be. We must be very careful indeed that no one should guess otherwise."

Letty clasped her hands and gripped them together tightly. "How soon will I see my brother, sir?" she asked, her eyes imploring, and he smiled again, to reassure her.

"In a matter of days, only," he declared. "The plan is that in three days from now, at a certain time in the evening, when all is dark, he will send us a signal light from a point farther down the coast, which has been most carefully pin-pointed by him and by myself. I will be waiting for his signal, and two of my most faithful retainers, both sworn to absolute secrecy, will row out with muffled oars to bring him aboard."

"Three days!" Letty repeated, joyfully. She turned back to the Rear-Admiral. "And what about my own appearance on the ship, sir?"

"That too has been arranged. Once your brother is safely aboard, and has resumed his own clothing and personality, you will keep out of sight until the following morning. Then the same trusted retainers will row ashore, presumably to spy out the land. You will by then have changed into feminine dress, and they will hide you beneath a tarpaulin in the boat, so that none of the sailors see you leaving the ship," he explained.

"Once ashore, you will be set on land, and will then have the second role which has been assigned to you to play. You must stagger out into the water, as though in the last stages of exhaustion, and beg them to help you — in English, of course. You will supposedly be a young English lady who is trying to escape from France to join her family in England. My men will bring you back to the Columbella in full view of all aboard, and your story will be told to them. What name do you wish to use for the deception, by the way? You cannot, obviously, use your own."

Letty went red. She wanted to use David's name, and pass herself off as a Miss Gray, so as to have at least that tiny link with him, but she saw that would be unwise.

"I shall be Miss — Miss Arabella Brown, if you think that suitable."

"The Rear-Admiral nodded. "Why not?" he said. "Right. Miss Arabella Brown it shall be. And once you have been tidied and have curled your hair and are attired as a lady, I'll warrant that none of my men will recognise the dashing Commander Fanshawe they have seen walking up and down for the last three days."

Here David intervened for the first time. "There is only one thing we must remember," he said quietly. "And that is that, even though Miss Fanshawe will be dressed as a lady, with her hair curled, and so on, there is a remarkable likeness between her and her twin brother."

The Rear-Admiral nodded again. "That too has been thought of," he told them. "We will put about the story that Miss — Miss Brown is too ill and exhausted even to take exercise, so none of the men will see her, not even at a distance, until I have made arrangements for a frigate to return her — and yourself, my good sir — to England. I doubt very much whether the wet and bedraggled female who is brought aboard will be connected in any way with a similarity to the Commander. Her hair will be darkened by the sea, for one thing, and tangled round her shoulders. No, I think we are safe there, and when she leaves the ship for the frigate, we will somehow procure a bonnet that hides most of her face."

"So I have only three days to carry out my impersonation," Letty said. "I do hope I wil be able to manage it. Mr Gray has told me some of the things I must do and will come to my aid if I am in difficulties."

"I too will see that you are not placed in any position where you might find yourself out of your depth," the Rear-Admiral promised her. "I will do all I can, and between us, we will carry it off." He paused, then added gravely, "You are an exceptional young lady, Miss Fanshawe."

★ ★ ★

The three days that followed seemed to Letty to pass very quickly and, to her great relief, David and the Rear-Admiral between them made things as easy as possible for her, answering when one of the men spoke to her, and simply allowing her to be seen. She hardly had to speak or give any orders. When she did speak, she tried to make her voice as much like Greville's as she could, but it was a strain, and each night, she tumbled exhausted into her bunk.

Much of the time, her thoughts were with Greville, carrying out his desperate mission. How she looked forward to seeing him again! But she had to admit that her main pre-occupation was with David Gray. Her eyes followed him about, and she longed for the chance to tell him of her love, but in the midst of their present circumstances, they had little chance, even when alone in their cabin, to talk of things other than the problems that had arisen because of Letty's deception.

His protectiveness lay over her like a cloak, however, and she revelled in his constant presence at her side. If only he loved her as she loved him! Added to her anxiety about Greville, and the strain of carrying out her part as her brother, was the ever-present question of whether he would tell her, perhaps on their way back to England, that she meant as much to him as he meant to her. She did not think she could bear it if he were to go casually out of her life once the adventure was over. But he had said, on their arrival, that once there was no danger, they could talk of their personal feelings, and often, she surprised a tender glance in his grey-green eyes, or a proud half-nod when she had carried out a particularly difficult task. He must love her! He must!

The third day was almost unbearable, and when at last dusk fell, Letty was keyed up to a pitch of anxiety that made it impossible for her to rest or eat. She paced back and forth in the tiny cabin, waiting for the Rear-Admiral to summon her and David so that they could all watch for Greville's signal together. David said nothing, but from time to time, he took her hand and pressed it encouragingly.

Then, at last, the summons came, a quick word from one of the Rear-Admiral's trusted retainers who were to row out and bring Greville aboard. Wrapping themselves in dark cloaks, David and Letty made their way in the dark up the steps to where the Rear-Admiral stood on the after-deck with his telescope; and they stood in a huddled little group.

Letty strained her eyes, but could see nothing except a mass of land, dark against the dark sky. There were no lights, and everywhere seemed absolutely deserted.

"We should see his signal in a few moments," the Rear-Admiral said in a low voice.

Letty leaned on the rail, her every sense alert. She was conscious of David beside her, and his rapid breathing as he too watched for the tiny flash of light from the shore. The boat was ready, its oars muffled, to bring Greville ashore, and was waiting in the shadow of the Columbella.

The seconds ticked past, and then Letty could restrain herself no longer. Are you certain this is the place?" she hissed.

"Absolutely," the reply came back. "There can be no mistake about that. But we must give him time. Perhaps he has been delayed."

So once again, silence descended on the little group, and Letty could hear the creaking and groaning of the vessel, the breeze in the rigging, the splash of the sea.

Moments passed, and again she whispered, "Perhaps he could not procure a lantern. Should not the boat row out to search for him?"

"No, he will have a lantern if he is there," the Rear-Admiral told her calmly.

"If he is there? What do you mean?" Letty demanded, beside herself with anxiety now.

"It may be that he is unable to signal tonight for some reason. We will give him another hour, and then wait until tomorrow. Those were the plans agreed upon," she was told.

She moaned, "An hour! I cannot wait an hour! Oh, where can he be?"

"He will come," was the reassuring reply.

But Greville did not come. There was no signal that night, and the hour crept past until the Rear-Admiral announced that they would have to wait now until the following night. Letty could have wept from frustration.

"Where can he be? What can have

happened?" she almost sobbed to David, once they were safely back in their small cabin, and he put his arms around her.

"Shhh, Letty. You must be very brave. Tomorrow, he will surely come. A hitch can occur with even the best-laid plans. Greville is depending on you for his life. You cannot give way now."

Letty managed, by a heroic effort, to quieten her sobs. "But now I must get through yet another day," she said in desperation, and he put his head down to her hair, so that his lips touched her lightly.

"Yes, you must. But you can. And you will. And I am here, as I promised. You're not alone."

"Oh, David, whatever should I do without you?" Letty whispered, her own arms reaching up to surround him, and they stood for some moments in a close embrace. Then David gently released himself.

"Sleep, darling," he told her, leading her to her bunk and helping her off with her coat. "You need all the sleep you can get to go through the strain of tomorrow."

Without another word, he extinguished the candle of the lantern, and she heard him climb into his own bunk. No time now to think of donning nightshirts, the dawn was far too near. But in the darkness, Letty was calmed and even happy.

He called me 'darling', she thought over and over to herself, as she drifted peacefully off to sleep.

★ ★ ★

The tension of the next day communicated itself to all three of them; Letty, David and the Rear-Admiral. They went about with pursed lips and strained expressions. By the time night came, Letty was once again strung up to a feverish pitch, but she was more hopeful. Tonight he could come and the waiting would be over.

Once more, the ship had taken up

its position and, at the appointed time, the three of them in dark cloaks, stood breathlessly waiting and watching the shore for the glimmer of light that would tell them Greville had been successful in his mission.

"He is late again," the Rear-Admiral muttered, worry in his voice. "Pray God nothing has gone wrong."

"Wait — wait. He may have been delayed," David's calm voice reassured them, but Letty felt the first stirrings of dread, like a cold touch at the back of her neck.

He was not going to come. All of a sudden, she knew it. She was Greville's twin and, at times of difficulty, there had always been a sort of invisible bond between them. It was as though their thoughts reached out to each other, and she seemed to sense her brother now, trying desperately to tell her that all was not right; that his mission had failed and he was in danger — deadly danger and needed her help.

She sent her own thoughts, her own

strength, out into the void, hoping he would sense that she had received his message.

Then she turned to the two men. "He is not going to come," she said calmly, now that she knew the worst, and knew what she had to do. "I can tell. I am his twin, and we have a bond between us. I hear him telling me that he has failed, that he is in danger. He is calling to me for help. I must go to him."

"But there is still time, the hour has not yet passed," the Rear-Admiral protested.

Letty shrugged in the dark. "Wait then. But it will do no good. I can pass the time in making my plans."

At the end of an hour, even the Rear-Admiral had to admit that something must be wrong, for no light showed itself, and he said in deep concern, "We had better all go to my cabin."

Once in the privacy of his richly-appointed suite, he turned to Letty. "Well, Miss Fanshawe, it appears that you were right. Something is indeed wrong — though even now, your brother may be making his way towards the coast."

"No, he is in danger somewhere. In Paris, I think," Letty said slowly, concentrating hard on Greville's image in her mind. "He is calling to me for help, and I am going to go to him. I have it all planned now. Luckily, I speak French, though only in a school-girl fashion. I can always pretend to be a little simple in the head, though, if things become too difficult."

Resolutely she faced the Rear-Admiral. "I hope you will assist me, sir. I require the tattered gown I was to have worn as Arabella Brown, and whatever you can spare me in the way of money and food. I must go to Greville, and save him."

The Rear-Admiral gasped incredulously. "Do you realise what you are proposing to do, ma'am? To go alone into an enemy country, and try to find your brother somewhere in Paris. It will be like looking for a needle in a haystack! I cannot allow you to do such a dangerous thing. In fact, I positively forbid it!"

Letty stood her ground. "Then I shall have to manage without your assistance, sir," she declared. "For I am determined to go. If I might just have the gown, please. I cannot expect to get anywhere dressed as an officer of His Brittanic Majesty's Navy."

"Mr Gray, say something to her! Make her see how foolish her plan is," the Rear-Admiral expostulated.

David quietly took Letty's hand, and turned with grave eyes. "She means what she says, sir, and you will help her by giving her as much assistance as possible. And she will not be going alone. I will be with you," he said to Letty, clasping her hand tightly. "I speak fluent French, and you may need a man to protect you."

Letty's eyes began to shine suspiciously with tears. "Oh, David!" was all she could say.

Once her plan had been made, Letty insisted that she and David should act at once.

"We must go now, tonight, in the boat that you had waiting to bring Greville ashore, sir," she told the Rear-Admiral. "I am afraid you will have to think of some way to explain our absence in the morning."

"Oh, I can do that readily enough. And I shall have your brother's sea-chest and Mr Gray's baggage safely hidden so that it will seem as though you have really left the ship," Sir Charles told her, all his concern now on seeing that she received as much help as he could possibly give her.

She was presented with the clothes that had been intended for her role as the desperate Arabella Brown and, in the privacy of her cabin, she changed from Greville's man's attire into the petticoat and gown, which had been torn and tattered to assist the illusion that the lady who begged for assistance had been through some

60

desperate adventures.

While she continued her preparations, combing out her hair so that it hung in flaxen waves to her shoulders, only a little shorter now than it had once been, and putting on the stockings and slippers that had been provided, David, in the rear-Admiral's cabin, was engaged in altering his own appearance in a similar manner.

"We must look like two gipsies — but not too disreputable," he remarked to Sir Charles, who was busily collecting together a large amount of money, which he placed in a money-belt, telling David to strap it round his waist.

"That should ensure you manage for as long as necessary," the Rear-Admiral declared. "Now, you will want food."

He called one of his two trusted servants, who had been aware of the original plan, and hastily explained to him what had happened, and what Letty and David intended to do.

The man scratched his head. "If

they're to be gipsies, sir, begging your pardon, they should have their food and drink wrapped in bundles. And maybe they should carry something. Gipsies usually do something as they wander from place to place. They dance, or play tunes, or — "

"A fiddle!" David interrupted, with sudden inspiration. "I can play the violin. I have never tried to pass myself off as a gipsy with a fiddle, but it should not be too difficult," he smiled. "And Miss Fanshawe will have to abandon all her gentility and dance. That too should not prove too much for her. A few twirls of her skirt, a few claps of the hands, and dance steps should suffice. She will learn. She is quick and capable."

"Can you procure these things, Evans?" the Rear-Admiral asked.

The man winked and touched the side of his nose with one finger. "I has me methods, sir, begging your pardon again," he promised, and disappeared.

At last, the little group gathered in

the Rear-Admiral's cabin. Letty had torn off the bottom of the tattered skirt, and her pretty ankles and slippers showed. David was wearing rough pantaloons and a shirt and jerkin. Evans was there, and laid the objects he was carrying on the table, while David explained to Letty his idea that they should pass themselves off as two wandering gipsies.

She thought the plan was excellent, and even managed a smile when he told her, rather apologetically, that she would have to dance a little to keep up the pretence.

"I'll dance. Don't worry, I can do it. I've been to many celebrations in the villages at home, and I know how to do a gipsy dance," she explained, adding, "though I've never had the chance until now. It was not considered suitable for the 'Young Lady from the Big House' to join in such frivolities."

"Well, here's my fiddle," David said, picking it up, and placing it in position, though he did not draw the bow across the strings. "And what's this? A little drum?"

"For the young lady to sling across her shoulder, sir, when you're calling the passers-by to watch the show and throw you money," Evans explained. "She can beat it to gain attention."

"Good, splendid," David approved, and Letty at once slung the drum across her shoulder to be carried away when they left.

"And here's your bundle, sir," Evans said finally, as David picked up a stick, to which was attached a large bundle wrapped in a spotted cloth. "Food and drink, and a few small things you might need."

"I can't thank you enough. You've done wonders," David said impulsively.

"I shan't forget this night's work, Evans," the Rear-Admiral told him. "Now, that seems to be all. Have you a plan of where you are going to set out for?" he asked David, who nodded.

"We'll head for Rennes, and there

we may be able to procure horses, or change our clothes for something better. Perhaps even take seats on a coach, if one is passing through in the direction of Paris," he said.

"Greville will guide us, of that I am sure," Letty declared, with certainty.

"Then it only remains for me to wish you good luck and Godspeed, ma'am," the Rear-Admiral said formally, bowing over her hand. "Mr Gray thinks you should be back here within about two weeks. So, two weeks from now, the Columbella will be awaiting your signal. In the meantime, I will send at once to the Admiralty to inform them what has happened."

"Thank you, sir," Letty replied, with dignity. She turned. "The boat is ready? Then I think we should go."

4

LETTY awoke from a deep, exhausted sleep to find the sun slanting into her eyes, and she sat up hastily. David was curled up beside her. They had spent the remainder of the night, after they had been rowed ashore and had scrambled as far away from the cliff-edge as they could until they collapsed from exhaustion, in some farmer's field, amid the growing crops. A blanket, which Evans had pushed into her hands at the last moment, had provided a bed for them, and with no thought of propriety, she and David had huddled up together for warmth, and fallen asleep immediately.

Now, as she looked across at his face, with the grey-green eyes hidden by long, blond lashes, and his fair hour tousled, her love for him swelled almost unbearably in the breast. Dear David! To risk his own life to come with her in search of Greville! How could she ever do enough to pay him back for his protection and care?

She longed to lean over and kiss his sleeping face awake, but only a few seconds after she had sat up, he moved also, and his eyes, alert at once, took in their situation.

He turned to her and smiled. "So we have been sleeping in a cabbage patch! Let us hope the farmer does not catch us. We must eat now, to keep our strength, before trying to find our way to Rennes."

Letty shook back her hair, and tried to tidy it with her hands, while he unwrapped their bundle, and revealed cheese and fruit, and a bottle of some dubious-looking drink, which turned out, after a cautious sip, to be rum and water.

While they ate, David continued speaking. "We must decide what our relationship is to be, for it may prove embarrassing otherwise. For who but a man and wife would sleep together in a cabbage patch? Yet we cannot pass as man and wife. I do not think it would be wise. I suggest brother and sister. And we will be of foreign extraction, not native French. You shall be called Lola, and I will take the name of Louis. I fear I am not familiar with gipsy names. But how does the plan sound so far?"

Letty, her mouth full of apple, nodded her approval. Then she proclaimed, "Lola and Louis, 'the Wandering Gipsies,' dance and fiddle for your delight. Yes I think we could get away with that. And, of course, as gipsies, we will carry no papers, though we may find ourselves in difficulties because we have nothing to show who we are. Still, I think we could bluff our way through."

David was wrapping the remains of their breakfast together in the spotted cloth. "One thing — we must never speak in English unless we are absolutely certain we cannot be overheard," he said seriously.

She nodded. "I had already thought of that. And so, *mon brave, Vive la France!*"

★ ★ ★

They set off along a rough track through the fields.

"Paris is eastwards, so we must go by the sun to begin with," David said. He looked round the deserted landscape, the fields and the trees. "But the first person we come across, we will ask the way to Rennes."

"There's somebody now," Letty breathed, pointing, and following her gaze, he saw a rough cart making its way towards them, being pulled by a little donkey. An old man sat at the reins.

"Let's go across to him," David whispered, and they made their way across a field to the cart, which stumbled to a stop as the old man saw them. On reaching him, they discovered he was not as old as they had imagined. His face was weatherbeaten, with wise eyes of a brilliant blue, which looked them over calmly.

"Pardon me," David began in French. "But could you tell us the way to Rennes?"

"Why do you want to go to Rennes?" was the unexpected reply.

David shrugged. "It seems the quickest way to reach Paris. We are on our way to Paris," he explained, and the man was silent, while his brilliant, blue eyes examined them both.

Then he said, to Letty's horror, "You will never deceive anyone without help, you know. Forgive my English, it is not very good. But whatever you are pretending to be, even I, Jacques Lemain, can see that you are both English."

"Oh, my God!" Letty breathed, her hand going to her mouth, and her whole body becoming chilled. Were they to fail even before they had set out on their mission?

"I am correct, am I not?" the old man asked, in English, and David looked helplessly at Letty. In that moment when their eyes met, she seemed to hear Greville's voice saying, 'Tell him, Letty! Tell him!'

Resolutely, she faced the older man. "Yes, Monsieur Lemain, you are right. We are on our way to Paris to try to rescue my brother, who is in some sort of danger."

"*Merci, mam'selle*," Jacques said, with a little bow. He smiled suddenly. "My farm is just over there. Let us all go together. No doubt you would find food and drink agreeable?"

"But what are you going to do?" David demanded desperately. "Are you going to hand us over to the authorities?"

Jacques turned a vivid blue glance upon him. "The authorities? I spit on the authorities! *Non, monsieur*, at my farm we will make the plans — how I can help, how I can get you to Paris unsuspected, and rescue the young man who is in danger."

And, for the first time in her life, Letty fainted from sheer relief.

★ ★ ★

Letty came to her senses to be aware, at first, of a series of comforting smells: onions, garlic, apples, hot chocolate, delicious vegetable broth. She opened her eyes, and looked dazedly round to see that she was in a low-beamed, farm kitchen; lying on a settle, her head cradled in David's lap. She sighed, a sigh of pure pleasure, and wished she could stay there for ever, in the pleasant surrounds of the kitchen, with David's arm beneath her head.

He bent over her. "Are you all right now? You fainted. It's all this strain, it has been too much for you."

A voice spoke from across the room, the wise old voice of Jacques. "The little one will be recovered once she has had some of Sophie's broth, and a hot drink with cognac in it. Can you sit up now, my child, and Sophie will give you the broth?"

Letty struggled to sit up. She felt light-headed but very much at home in this friendly house. A plump, motherly woman took David's place beside her and began to spoon broth into her mouth. It was delicious, and after a few mouthfuls, Letty protested that she could manage the spoon herself. She ate ravenously until the bowl was empty. Then a mug containing hot chocolate and cognac was thrust into her hands.

Jacques, who was sitting in a rocking chair with his pipe, chuckled as she drank. "I think she will live," he said in French.

David was being served at the table by the motherly Sophie, and he too seemed much better for the good food.

"What has happened? Have you explained who we are?" Letty asked him, speaking without fear in English, knowing that they were among friends.

He nodded. "Jacques knows all about your brother, and your determination to go to Paris to rescue him. He is going to come with us, and help us. We've been discussing it while you lay in a faint."

"And Sophie?" Letty asked.

"Jacques' wife. She will run the farm, with the help of his brother, while he is away," David explained. "And she is going to provide us with more suitable clothes. We must be dressed properly, Jacques says, or the authorities will be certain to know that something is wrong."

"But why? Why are you doing this for us?" Letty asked, turning her eyes on the old man.

He shrugged. "I love my country, the beautiful France," he said slowly, in English. "And to see and hear what we have seen and heard in these last few years — our King and Queen murdered, the land laid waste by pillaging and looting hordes, madmen in power — we, who live close to the earth, know that this is wrong. France is being bled to death, and only in corners such as this one, where we are too far from the troops and crazy hordes, is there still peace."

David told Letty calmly, "I have told Jacques that Greville risked his life to obtain information to assist our Admiralty against Napoleon. He wants to see peace in France, Letty, and he believes that we English can help to achieve it, even though most Frenchmen regard us as enemies now."

"All men should live as brothers," Jacques declared, and Letty knew that she and David had been lucky to come across such a good man.

"I can only say with all my heart, thank you — *merci, monsieur*," she offered softly.

He smiled at her, and inclined his head with gentle gravity. But then his mood changed. "While we are sitting here, your brother is in danger. We must take action at once. Sophie has clothes for you both, and I must make my arrangements for leaving for a while. Go and change into peasant dress. You must assume the identities of my son and his wife for our journey."

"But — Letty began, thinking of their carefully-laid plans for being gipsies.

David said carefully, "it may be rather awkward for us to pretend to be a man and his wife. Is there no other way? Could we not be brother and sister?"

Jacques gave them a long look, then his wise old eyes twinkled suddenly. "But why should it be difficult for you to act the parts of married people? You are in love with each other, am I not right?"

Letty gazed at the floor and blushed, while David appeared tongue-tied, and also reddened. They glanced at each other, then away again.

"*Alors*, but it is obvious that you adore each other. When you return to England, you would be married," Jacques went on, busy with his pipe, and enjoying their discomfiture. "So we make a small stop on our journey. Not far away lives the Abbé Montpelier. He shall marry you by the rights of Holy Church, then you will indeed be man and wife."

"I will fetch my mother's ring," the delighted Sophie cried, in French, and she hurried from the room.

David and Letty turned to each other, very slowly. Letty's eyes were darkened to emerald, and shone like stars. David's face was full of tender adoration and passion.

Oblivious to Jacques, they stared at each other for a long moment, then David held out his arms.

"Letty, could you ever — would you?"

"Oh, my darling, my darling," Letty cried, and then he was holding her and covering her face with kisses, while she clung to him as though she would never let him go.

"So that is settled," Jacques remarked calmly. "Go now, and put on the clothes Sophie has ready for you. Then we will set off. And our first stopping place shall be at the dwelling of my old friend, the Abbé."

* * *

As she washed in the soft rain-water in the basin on the wash-stand, then slid into the French, peasant dress with its flounced skirt of dark red, Letty was thinking to herself, in disbelief, "I am preparing for my wedding! This will be my wedding dress!"

Sabots on her feet, bare legs, and her hairbrushed into a soft cloud round her face, she emerged, shyly, into the tearful embrace of Sophie, who presented her with a small handful of wild flowers. The motherly woman, in her delight at a wedding, twined some of the flowers into Letty's flaxen locks, and gave her the rest to hold. Smilingly, she led Letty to a mirror, and the girl beheld herself transformed, joy radiating from her as she stood in the short-skirted peasant dress, with her wedding bouquet of wild flowers.

David, looking for all the world like a French peasant farmer, but an unbelievably handsome one, was waiting for her, and the same joy was written upon his countenance.

"You make the loveliest bride I have ever seen, my darling," he told her, taking her hand, and added, "but Jacques is waiting. We must go."

They kissed Sophie good-bye, and Jacques assisted Letty on to the seat of the cart, which was waiting with the little donkey in the shafts. A horse stood saddled, but Jacques told David to lead her rather than ride her, for the Abbé's house was only a short distance away. Later, he would ride beside the cart. Then, in the softly golden afternoon sunshine, they set off . . .

It was like a wonderful dream. Letty sat as the Abbé, a rotund figure, in his clerical black robe, was summoned from his house and Jacques spoke to him in rapid French. Then the Abbé turned to smile at the young couple.

"He says, if you go into the church and wait, he will be ready in a few moments," Jacques told them.

So together, hand in hand, Letty and David entered the tiny, country church, where the lamps flickered dimly, and the sweet eyes of the statue of the Madonna gave them a blessing.

In the cool, calm interior, they sat with bowed heads, each unable to believe the fortune that had brought them here so unexpectedly. Neither of them was a Roman Catholic, nor understood the Catholic service, but here in this little, homely church, it didn't seem to matter.

When the Abbé came in, the dignity of his calling like a cloak about him, they stood, and as he spoke the words that would unite them, and Jacques gave the responses, and told them what to say, Letty thought she would never forget this moment — her wedding. So very different from the sort of wedding she had expected to have some day, and so much more beautiful.

David produced Sophie's mother's ring, and at the Abbé's instructions, slid it on to Lettty's finger. It was only very slightly too large, and the thick, heavy band of gold, glossy with the patina of age, looked as though it had been made especially for her slender hand.

Then, at last, it was over, a simple, beautiful ceremony of which they had understood scarcely a word, but which had made them man and wife. David kissed Letty's lips very tenderly, and the Abbé smilingly invited them to take a drink of wine at his little house to celebrate their union.

"He would be offended if we did not," Jacques said, and they both agreed that the last thing they wanted to do was to offend the cheerful little man who had married them.

As they sipped their wine, Letty very conscious of the heavy ring nestling upon her finger, David asked, "but shouldn't there be some sort of record of our marriage?"

"The Abbé will see to it," Jacques reassured him, and added, "all he requires is your full names and places of residence. And you have no need to worry. No authorities would ever think of searching the records of a tiny country church for proof that two English people were married here." he smiled. "So! Now you can play the parts of my son and daughter-in-law, eh?" Gerard and Solange Lemain."

"Things are happening so fast, I can hardy keep up with them," David said wryly.

Jacques' eyes had grown grim. "We must not forget, even in your happiness, the young man in Paris. Straight away, once we have left the Abbé, we start on our journey. Tell me, what money do you have?"

"Gold, plenty of it," David assured him, and Jacques looked dubious.

"Peasants do not possess gold. Show it to no one, but if you will give me a few of the coins, they will help to assist our path to Paris." he hesitated, then went on, "During the Reign of Terror, we had a system by which many of the aristocrats were passed across France, from one place of safety to another, until they could take ship for England. I am counting on the fact that the members of our chain of safety will assist you to find the young man, and smuggle him, too, away from Paris.

"I will not be with you all the time, you will be passed on to other trustworthy men who will help you. We do not go through the towns and cities, we take the short cuts that only the men who have lived there for many years know of. But rest assured, you should be in Paris within three days, or four at the most."

"But then we must find Greville, and it is only Letty's intuition that tells us he is there somewhere. I have no idea where to start looking for him," David admitted, worriedly.

"Do not fear. We have our own ways of finding information. If he is in Paris, you will reach him safely," Jacques told him.

Then he turned to the Abbé. "I am afraid I must take them away now."

The Abbé nodded, and in a moment of solemnity, held out his hands to bless Letty and David, and wish them success in their venture.

Then he shook Jacques' gnarled fist, and held it for a moment, before coming outside to watch them climb into the cart; Letty and Jacques on the seat, and David mounted on the sturdy horse that trotted alongside, gentle and obedient to his every touch.

In the golden afternoon, the little party moved off, and the Abbé stood with the breeze fluttering his robes, waving until he was only a far-off speck in the distance.

★ ★ ★

The cart rumbled on through the hours of the late afternoon and early evening, and twilight began to creep over the countryside. Letty thought, rather dubiously, that she might find she had some bruises in rather unmentionable places after being bumped about so much, and envied David the comfort of his horse's saddle.

Her heart swelled with pride whenever she looked at him, riding along beside them. Many times on that journey, their glances met, and they smiled at each other. She could still hardly believe it. That she was now Mrs David Gray. She looked down at the ring upon her finger, and felt so happy she thought she would float off into the soft, violet twilight with joy.

They seemed to go on for miles, and Jacques took them through short cuts and tracks which avoided the main thoroughfares. They had passed few dwellings, and had seen few people, but at length, just as it was becoming almost too dark to carry on, a little hamlet came into view through the trees, with lights twinkling in the cottages.

Jacques passed through the cluster

of small houses, and went on along a track that led them to a farm, where he announced, "And here we are."

He left them standing together beside the cart, David's arm protectively around Letty, while he went to the door and knocked. When the door opened, they saw a burly figure outlined against the firelight from within, and there was the sound of quick French conversation. Then Jacques returned and ushered David and Letty towards the door, which still stood open.

"My old friend and comrade, Monsieur Regnier," he said, as they shyly entered the huge farm kitchen, so like Jacques' own.

A huge man, smiling warmly, seized their hands in a rough clasp of friendship, and said in halting English, "You are welcome in my house. My wife is preparing a room. I understand that this is your bridal night?"

"Yes, Monsieur," Letty admitted, rosy blushes suffusing her face.

"Then you shall have a true bridal chamber to rest after your journey," the farmer told them. "But first, you sit, yes, and my daughter will give you food and drink."

When David and Letty had finished eating, and were feeling they could not possibly manage another crumb, a small woman in a white apron came bustling into the room.

"Your bridal chamber — it is ready," the farmer told them, smiling, and introduced his wife, who beamed, just as Sophie had done, over the prospect of a newly-married couple sleeping beneath her roof.

She led them to a long, low room with a comfortable-looking bed covered with a patchwork quilt. Hot water and towels were ready on the wash-stand. A lamp was burning, and the room looked fresh and scrubbed and utterly irresistible. The farmer's wife had even placed a bowl of fresh flowers on the chest.

They entered the room, David's hand

closed in Letty's, where the wedding ring caught the light and gleamed.

"*Bon nuit, mes enfants.*" The good lady smiled, and shut the door firmly behind them.

5

PARIS! Letty stood with David's arm around her, bemused by the first sight of the hustle and bustle of the streets, the tall buildings, the slender threads of church steeples piercing the sky, and the other craft on the mighty river where Lucien's barge, with its cargo of fresh vegetables, was gliding into the ancient city.

Somewhere here, she was thinking, amid the noise and stink, glamour and squalor, was Greville. She could almost feel his presence near her. Soon, they would find him.

As Lucien, the dark, handsome boatman, who had carried them in his barge on the last slow stage of their journey, stood busy avoiding other craft, Letty thought over the events of the past few days; since she and David had been married in the little country church that now seemed so far away.

They had travelled many miles, they had passed through forests, fields, hills, valleys. They had seen some of the once glorious chateaux which had been burned and pillaged during the reign of Terror, with windows gaping and smoke-blackened walls. They had ridden, once Jacques handed them over to the next person who was to see them on the safe way into Paris, for miles and miles, until Letty was exhausted, while the cheery Georges sang as they rode, in a fruity bass, the songs of his country and old folk-ballads.

They had spent two nights in the homes of strangers, who had welcomed them with the same warmth all these people who made up the chain of safety had shown, and one night in the fragrance of a pile of hay in a barn. And then Georges had brought them to the river, and placed them in the care of Lucien, who had promised to deliver them safely to comrades in Paris where they could stay while they searched for Greville.

Now, here they were, perhaps only hours away from him. Letty's heart began to hammer in her breast. Then, even as she wondered how they should go about their search, Lucien called out to a passing barge, and began to steer towards where a flight of steps descended to the murky waters of the river. He secured the barge to an iron ring, and came to Letty and David.

"Here you leave my boat," he said, in a low voice, though it was doubtful whether anyone else could have heard him above the sounds of the open market; where early housewives were bargaining for the wares being brought in by the bargees from the country districts around. "I will summon one of my friends to see to the business that has brought me here, while I take you to the man and his wife whose house is where you will stay. Wait for me a moment."

He bounded up the flight of steps from the barge, while Letty seated herself on a sack full of vegetables, and they saw him, make his way amid the crowds.

David sat down beside Letty and took her hand. "We have been very lucky, he said. "Our meeting with Jacques might have been with anybody — an enemy, even, who would have handed us straight over to the authorities."

"Yes, it is true," Letty agreed, giving a slight shudder as, for the first time, she caught sight of the uniforms of soldiers amid the crowds in the market.

Then Lucien hailed them from the steps, in French. "My old friend will take care of selling my produce for me. Come, cousins, and I will show you where Jean-Paul and his wife live."

"No need!" cried another voice, also in French, and they all turned to see a grey-haired man with a buxom beauty beside him, making their way through the crush. The man was smiling. "I couldn't wait to see your cousins, Lucien, so we decided to come and meet you, did we not, Denise?"

David rose to his feet, but Letty was unable to move a muscle.

An icy hand seemed to grip her heart, and she could hear Greville's voice pounding in her head, over and over, 'Danger, Letty, danger! Enemies! Enemies!'

Her brain acted of it own volition and, as she began to stand, she swayed, as though overcome with faintness, and allowed herself to collapse in what she hoped was a convincing heap on the wooden boards of the barge.

Immediately, David bent over her, while Lucien came rushing down the steps. But before he was within hearing distance, Letty hissed in David's ear; "These people are not friends, but enemies. Greville's trying to warn me, I'm sure of it. Keep us away from them and tell Lucien."

Then she allowed herself to be lifted like a doll in David's strong arms, and carried into the cabin; where he laid her gently down on the bunk.

Then Lucien came striding into the

cabin, bending his head as he entered through the low doorway. "What is it?" he asked David. "Is she all right?"

Letty kept her eyes shut and her breathing even.

"That man and the woman, they mean harm to us, and Letty's brother is warning her to keep away from them; he is her twin, and they have a sort of bond of thought between them," David explained swiftly.

Lucien frowned. "Jean-Paul was always a member of the chain of safety, and yet, I've never really been quite at ease in his company. He may have turned traitor since the Reign of Terror," he muttered. "What shall I say? They are coming on board."

"Tell them we think it's a fever, but we'll come to their house later. In the meantime, send someone you can trust to their house to spy out the land," David whispered, thinking fast. He could hear the sound of the grey-haired man and Denise clambering into the barge, and then coming into the

94

cabin, where Denise pushed her way to Letty's side, and Jean-Paul hovered in the doorway.

"Poor child!" Denise crooned, lifting Letty's wrist and chafing her hand. "Why are you men standing around like idiots? Get her some cold water, or brandy — "

Letty gave a deep sigh and fluttered her eyelids open. "Oh!" she moaned.

"There, there, *cherie*. All the excitement of the journey and your visit to Paris has been too much for you," Denise declared. "But when we get you home, I will take care of you."

David put his arm round Letty's shoulders, as she struggled to sit up, and Lucien held a mug of something to her lips.

"I think it may be the fever she has," Lucien said, exchanging a glance with David. "Look how hot she is, and how she shakes."

"Fever?" Denise shrilled, moving hastily away. "Then it might be the forerunner of something contagious."

"Yes, now I think of it, she has been in contact with some sailors whose mates had died from typhoid," David added, in a worried tone.

Denise paled and gripped her husbands's arm.

"We cannot think of letting her come to you until we are certain she is really recovered, and it was just an ordinary swoon," Lucien told Jean-Paul, with seeming frankness. "Return home, and later, when she is better, and we are sure it is nothing serious, I'll bring them to you, dear friends. We cannot thank you enough for your help, but we do not want to expose you to infection."

Jean-Paul seemed to be wrestling with himself. At last, he said reluctantly, "Yes, perhaps that would be best. But, as soon as you are sure, our home is waiting to hide them while they search for the young man here in Paris."

"I know," Lucien said, and gripped Jean-Paul's hand. Then, with Denise almost dragging him from the boat,

Jean-Paul muttered a farewell phrase. He and his wife made their way to the steps and, while David and Lucien watched tensely, the two disappeared from view.

Letty sat up as the men turned. Have they gone?" she whispered in English. "Oh, thank God! I'm sure they mean us terrible harm and that something is waiting for us at their house. Lucien, is there someone you can send, quickly, who will get there ahead of them and find out what it is?"

The handsome young man pondered, then nodded.

"Send him straight away," Letty insisted.

So, without further questions, their friend strode from the cabin.

Letty seized David's hands and pulled him down to sit beside her. She leaned against his shoulder and was comforted, as his arm went round her.

"We are in danger, I know it, and when Lucien comes back, we must find some safe place to hide. For if the authorities know we are in Paris — "

As her voice trailed off, David gripped her shoulder. "Don't worry, my darling. Lucien will arrange something for us. He is a true and faithful friend."

His words were proved true when Lucien reappeared a few moments later, and told them, in English, "I have sent Pierre le Grand. He will be there and back in no time." He sat on the other bunk and shook his head. "Jean-Paul did not marry Denise until very recently. I think she is a bad influence on him. The rest of the members of the chain of safety must be warned, and you — I must find somewhere else for you to go. I think Pierre will have an idea or two, perhaps, when he returns.

★ ★ ★

They waited tensely but it didn't seem long before an odd, croaking voice spoke from the doorway, where Pierre le Grand had silenty appeared. Letty and David were both taken aback when they saw him, for 'le Grand' had led them to believe Lucien's friend would be a huge, burly man. Instead he was a dwarf, with a hunched back, and a wizened face.

He spoke and they all turned. "Somebody has magic powers, or a nose for danger sure enough."

"You've been to their house? What did you find out?" Lucien demanded.

The dwarf grinned. "Crawling with soldiers. They know there are two English spies in Paris, but they don't want to make a fuss by arresting them in public. The plan was, to grab them as soon as they went in through Jean-Paul's door. And they know why you two — " he nodded at Letty and David, "are here. They're using the young man as bait. Somebody's told the whole story. Jean-Paul and that shrew of a wife of his. You're all going to have to watch your step in future."

Since he spoke in such colloquial French, Letty hardly understood a word of what he said, but David and Lucien looked at each other in dismay.

"What is it?" Letty asked hesitantly.

"The French authorities know we are here, for Greville," David told her. "They are waiting to arrest us at the house of that man and his wife." He put his arm protectively around her, and asked Pierre, "Will they come here for us, do you think, when Jean-Paul and his wife return without us?"

The dwarf shrugged.

"What do you suggest, Pierre?" Lucien asked. "The chain of safety must perform this last service before it is disbanded for ever. These two must rescue the young man, and be returned safely to Brest, where their ship is waiting to take them to England." He lifted a hand and clenched his fist. "Thank God Jean-Paul was only told they were coming to Paris to find the young lady's brother — and he does not know how they made their way here or how they will escape, nor that they must get to Brest. But they do not even know where her brother is . . . "

"In prison," the dwarf told them calmly, inspecting his nails. "An old prison used by the French Admiralty. And you can be certain that everyone employed there will be alerted for the English spies who may try to help him escape. A member of his own chain of safety turned traitor on him, and he was arrested as he was leaving Paris."

"In prison? Greville is in prison?" Letty gasped. She had managed to pick up the word in the dwarf's speech. She sat down suddenly. "How can we rescue him, David? It is a hopeless task, and yet, we must! We cannot leave him!"

"And the soldiers may be here at any time," Lucien added, reminding them of their own danger. "I must move the barge, at once. Never mind the produce, it was only an excuse to bring you here today, let it rot. I'll go and get the barge going, and we'll find another mooring place.

"Wait," the dwarf commanded, suddenly serious. He looked round at the other three. "Get your things together," he told Letty and David. "You're coming with me. And you, Lucien, be at the steps tomorrow night, to pick them up. And the young man."

"What do you mean?" David asked.

"Why, that I'm going to see you safely through this mission of yours," the dwarf replied casually. "I'll get the young man out of prison, and make certain the lot of you are packed off with Lucien back towards Brest tomorrow night. Now, come on, do as I say and hurry. Every moment counts, and the sooner I've got you in the back alleys of Paris, and Lucien has taken the barge away from here, the better."

They looked at each other, then all three of them set to work, carrying out his instructions with feverish activity.

6

EVEN in the sunlight of the morning, the alleys along which Pierre le Grand scuttled with Letty and David at his heels were dim, filthy, and filled with unpleasant smells.

He turned once, and gave them an impudent grin. "The soldiers won't venture into this part of Paris to look for two English spies, you can be sure of that," he croaked, and gave an earthy chuckle. Letty couldn't understand very much of what he said, as it was in quick colloquial French, but David pressed her hand reassuringly, and grinned back at the dwarf.

Further and further into the labyrinth of narrow alleys they went until, at last, Pierre stopped and told them, "We're home."

"Home?" Letty looked round her,

and almost screamed with horror and revulsion. They had stopped outside the ruins of what could only have been a charnel-house, and she could see bones tumbling in untidy heaps. She clung to David, and pressed her face against his shoulder.

He held her close, and asked Pierre, "Must she really be subjected to this? She's a delicately brought up young lady."

"She wants to live, doesn't she?" the dwarf rasped, but he pulled at Letty's sleeve and she looked shudderingly down at him.

"I beg your pardon, madame," he said, trying to make his voice gentle. "Do not be afraid. There is nothing here that will hurt you. But we outcasts of Paris must be certain of safety, and where better than a ruined crypt next to a charnel-house? Here, among the rogues and rascals of Paris, I guarantee, you will find only friendship. And the people you are going to meet will help you to save your brother, and take you

to safety. No one here will betray you."
He grinned at her. "Come, madame,
Will you accept my word that you are
welcome here — and safe?"

By now, Letty had regained command
of herself, and she met his gaze
squarely. "I am sorry, Pierre. It was
just the shock of seeing the bones,"
she told him, in her slow French. "I
cannot thank you enough for what you
are doing for us. I will come and meet
your friends gladly."

She and David held hands as Pierre
led them through the deep gloom of the
charnel-house, and through an archway,
down a flight of steel steps. He pounded
on the heavy wooden door that barred
their way, and called something in
hoarse French. From within, came
the sounds of many voices, and — to
Letty's surprise — a very savoury smell
of food cooking.

Then the door was flung open from
within, and they passed into one of the
strangest places Letty had ever seen in
her life.

It had formerly been a crypt, and there were pillars from the stone floor to the roof with its many carvings, grimed now by the smoke that rose from fires and candles that were burning against the dark. Little groups of people sat about here and there, and cauldrons were slung over some of the fires, being tended by figures which, from their bunched skirts and masses, of hair. Letty guessed were women.

She could not take in the whole scene at once. Her gaze roamed slowly over the men who sat, or lay on blankets on the stone floor, sleeping. One man had only half a face, the other half was a great mass of purple; another was so big and so powerful-looking that she shuddered to think what might happen if anybody should cross him — and yet, when she looked closer, she saw that his eyes were vacant, fixed on nothing with the stare of an idiot.

"Come," Pierre commanded. "I'll introduce you to our leader, Scarface, then you can share our meal. You'll need to rest afterwards, for tonight, once our plans are made, we must rescue your brother."

David held Letty's hand tightly, as they were solemnly introduced to the man with only half a face. He must have been handsome, once, Letty mused, for the one eye that looked back at her was as deeply blue as the sky and the hair that tumbled over the high forehead was a deep black. She felt a sudden stab of pity for a man who might have broken hearts by the dozen, and now was an object of horror, and her smile was genuine as she held out her hands to him, without prompting from David.

"Monsieur, I cannot express my thanks to you and your people for helping us," she said impulsively.

The twisted mouth smiled in a hideous travesty of a grin. But his voice was surprisingly attractive as he replied slowly, so that she would not misunderstand his French, "We creatures of the underworld may be thieves, pickpockets and ladies of the night, but, to our friends, we are loyal to death."

His one eye became thoughtful. "You are indeed a spirited young woman, madame," he touched the scarred side of his face. "Most girls would swoon at the sight of me. You have seen through the surface to the man beneath, and for that, I owe you thanks."

He turned to David and Pierre, who were standing close by in a little group. "Well, Pierre, and what has your agile brain devised for our plan of rescue tonight?"

"Let's sit down, and I'll tell you," the dwarf said, and they all pulled up some of the three-legged stools which were scattered about the crypt.

★ ★ ★

In the flickering light of the candles, Pierre spoke, and Letty listened hypnotised by his croaking voice and her surroundings.

"Simple enough," Pierre said, pulling

at his knuckles so that they cracked. "The young man is being held in the old Admiralty prison, together with others who are suspected of treason. It has a guard-room, where a Captain of the Police, one André Dubois, a young, but very efficient man is in charge of the guards. There is only one way out — through the guard-room."

Scarface's mouth twisted. "But you have thought of another way out, eh, Pierre?"

"Such a scheme had occurred to me," the dwarf said smugly. "But we'll need the help of the girls, and quite a few of the men, especially Hercule."

"Hercule?" David could not help querying, and the dwarf jerked a finger over his shoulder at the huge man, Letty had noticed, who sat with the fixed stare of an idiot.

"That's Hercule. He's as strong as twenty of the rest of us put together, though he has an addled brain. No need to feel sory for him, though. His needs are always taken care of. Like I told you, we help each other."

Letty leaned forward eagerly. "But what is your plan to rescue Greville?" she queried.

The dwarf grinned. "Those men on guard will be bored, especially during the night hours. Now don't you think they would appreciate it if some pretty girls were to walk in to keep them company, and have a few drinks with them?"

"But how will that help Greville?" Letty wanted to know.

"The men will be waiting hidden outside the prison," Pierre told her. "And it should be easy enough for one of the girls to find out which cell the young man is in. There are bars on cells, and Hercule can break bars like your good man here could crack a nut. The girls will make sure we have the right cell, and that there is enough noise going on in the guard-room to hide the sounds of the bars breaking, or coming free from their place. And once the bars have gone — "

"Greville can climb out?" Letty suggested, clasping her hands, her face ecstatic.

"If he can walk," the deep voice of Scarface put in, and they all turned to him. "Forgive me, madame, but he may have been badly treated during his time in the prison. That's where our men will help. If he is unable to walk, they must carry him. He may be unconscious, wounded, weak from hunger, but they will get him out, and bring him here. We will save him somehow.

Letty's hand went to her head suddenly. "David! Remember that dream I had on the ship!" she cried, horrified. "I saw Greville between soldiers, all bleeding, as if they had beaten him. It must have been real. Oh, God, I hope his injuries are not serious."

"Don't worry, madame," Scarface told her. "Our Old Mother Agnes can cure anything, and he will have food, a soft bed to rest on, whatever he requires."

"And by tomorrow night, he'll be ready to come with you to meet Lucien and get out of Paris, you'll see," Pierre assured her, seeing Letty's distress. "But what about the plan? Good, you think?"

"Excellent," Scarface pronounced, and he turned and called out for silence. The noise of chattering ceased, and the only sounds in the crypt were the crackling of the fires and the bubbling of the contents of the cauldrons, as every man and woman present waited for him to speak. In rapid French, he outlined what they would be required to do that night, and one of the women, a girl of about Letty's age, with long hair that fell in a tangled mass to her waist, gave a loud laugh.

"Oh, we can manage that all right, can't we, girls? Those guards won't know what's hit the guard-room."

The others joined in, swishing their skirts, and posing provocatively with hands on hips.

Only one of them, a sultry-looking brunette, came over and protested sulkily, "Why are you doing this for her, Scarface?"

The gang's leader put his arm about her waist in a familiar manner, and smiled lopsidedly. "No need for you to be jealous, my little she-cat. She has no designs on me. Can't you see that she is married to the gentleman with her — and that she is madly in love with him?"

Letty blushed. Surely the girl didn't think she was trying to steal Scarface's attentions for herself. Though, somehow, she wasn't surprised to learn that, even with his deformed face, he was still attractive to women and she was glad, for his sake, that girls still fought over his favours.

She went over to the girl, and held out her hand. "I do love my husband, and I wish for no other man in my life," she said, in the friendliest manner she could. "I promise you, we will be gone tomorrow, if all goes well. But you have no need to be jealous of me. In fact, I will need your help, and the help of all the rest of you, because I intend to come with you tonight into that guard-room."

"Letty!" David cried, overhearing her words. "Whatever are you thinking of? I forbid you to do such a foolish thing. What if you were caught?"

"Greville is my brother, David," Letty said quietly. "I cannot stand idly by while these kind people go to such lengths to save him. If I mix with the other girls — " she could not help the blush rising again, for she knew what sort of profession the 'girls' normally carried out, but she went on — "if I mix with them, they will see that I come to no harm, I am sure."

"She'll be safe enough with us," a blowzy blonde told David.

Then the gangleader's girlfriend unexpectedly declared, "I'll keep a personal eye on her myself. Don't worry, monsieur, we'll bring her back to you unharmed."

"Well, if you are going to go with the women, then I will go with the men," David said grimly. "Greville may need reassurance of what is happening, he will be glad to hear an English voice."

"So that's settled," Scarface said, spreading his hands in a Gallic gesture. "Now, surely the food is ready, Marie? Let us eat. And afterwards, our two friends must rest, ready for the night's work."

★ ★ ★

Surprisingly, the contents of the cauldrons proved to be a delicious stew, and Letty and David ate hungrily. Then Pierre, with hid malicious chuckle, led them to two straw pallets.

"Try to sleep," he said. "And don't worry," he added to David, with a leer. "You won't be robbed. All of us can smell money, and we know you're wearing a money-belt. But we don't rob our friends."

David, seated on one of the pallets, looked up into the dwarf's face in the flickering light. "I meant to speak to you about that," he said seriously. "People have been so kind to us that most of the money I was given for this undertaking has remained untouched. But you — and the rest of your people — are going to do such a great deal for us tonight, I feel it is only fair that you should receive some reward. Whom should I speak to — Scarface?"

"He looks after the money for us," Pierre acknowledged. "I'll bring him over."

The leader of the gang towered above David, who invited him to sit down, and explained what he had already said to Pierre.

"Let me give you some of the money I have," David went on. "You have been prepared to help us without payment, but life cannot be easy for any of you."

"It's true that we are the dregs of

the gutter, but we do well enough," Scarface told him, and his hideous smile twisted his mouth. "We are rich enough, *mon ami* — though the money does not come from the usual sources."

"All the same, I would like to make some gesture of thanks," David insisted.

The big man shrugged. "So be it. As you will."

David carefully removed his money-belt, and poured a handful of gold pieces into Scarface's fist."

"Will that be enough?" he asked.

The gang leader pressed his shoulder. "More than enough. Keep the rest of it, for you may need provisions and medical supplies for the young man. And you still have the journey back to the coast awaiting you. Who knows what difficulties you may encounter — and money, my friend, talks. A little bribery may mean the difference between life and death." He looked at David and his one eyebrow lifted quizzically. "Had it not occurred to you that if you had not been brought here by Pierre, your money-belt would have disappeared by now, without your even noticing it? Some of us have very light fingers."

David looked stunned, and Scarface rose from the pallet, amused.

"But don't fret," he said. "You have been accepted as one of us. The rest of your money is safe enough — or whoever tried to touch it will answer to me. But let this teach you a lesson, eh? When you wander the back alley of Paris, you are not safe unless you are beneath the protection of our organisation."

He sauntered off, and David turned to Letty, who had been watching with wide eyes.

He took her hand and said in a low voice, "I did not realise we were among such desperadoes."

"Don't worry on my account," Letty said. We have Scarface's word that we are beneath his protection. I am certain he would let none of them harm us.

But, oh, David, I am glad you are here. This place and these people — I have never imagined anything like them in my life."

"Let us hope we are never obliged to witness anyplace like this again, once we have left Paris," David said, and added tenderly, "But you must rest, love. We are forgetting why we are here, I shall not sleep, I'll just lie and watch over you. You'll need to be rested, and have your wits about you tonight, if we are to rescue Greville safely, and if you are determined to go into that guard-room with the others."

"They've said they will take care of me, love," she told him drowsily. "And I must go. I may even be able to help in some way."

She closed her eyes and, while he lay thinking dark thoughts about the coming events of the night, she slept peacefully in their ghastly surroundings, still holding his hand in her slumber.

★ ★ ★

Captain André Dubois was a sternly principled, very ambitious man of thirty, whose good looks had led many young ladies to flirt with him; but in vain. His whole interest lay in furthering his career, and in carrying out his duties to the best of his ability.

Tonight, as he strode into the guard-room of the old Admiralty prison, removing his immaculate gloves, he looked round with disdain. The naval men who were guarding the prisoners looked careless and unkempt. A few sharp words had them on their feet, their uniforms straightened, and the place made as tidy as possible. André was here to guard a political prisoner, as well as the rest who were incarcerated there, and he made an inspection of Greville's cell as soon as the guard-room was tidied up to his satisfaction.

The squalid cell, with its high, barred window, was filthy, and André's nose wrinkled fastidiously at the stench, as he looked down at the man who lay on the make-shift bed. Greville's blood-stained clothes clung to the wounds that had been inflicted upon him, and he had not washed or shaved for days. He was weak, but his eyes still held their glitter as he looked the Captain full in the face.

"Is there anything you require?" Andŕe asked in clipped tones.

Greville managed a crooked smile. "My freedom," he replied.

"You are a political prisoner," André told him. "You will be tried when — " Hastily, he bit off the words he had been about to say. He had almost revealed that the authorities were deliberately keeping Greville in prison, in the hope that the two English spies they knew were in Paris would make some attempt to rescue him, and fall into the net also. He clicked his heels and, with a brief bow, turned and left the cell. One of the guards turned the great key in the door behind him.

When he had gone, Greville sprang to his feet, his injured leg dragging as he went to the few stars that showed him the place of the window in the utter blackness. He reached out his hands and clasped the bars, his mind straining to it utmost in hope and fear.

She was nearby, he could almost feel her presence. Something was going to happen tonight, and Letty was sending him waves of cheer and hope in his lonely prison. In return, his own thoughts warned her, take care, little sister, take care! beware of the Captain he is the one to fear! Tread carefully — beware of the Captain! Take care!

7

IT was past midnight. The candles were guttering, and the prison guards were desultorily playing cards or dice. They yawned and wished the young Captain would leave them and go into his private office, so that at least they could relax and maybe snatch a wink of sleep.

Everything was quiet in the prison. There was no sign of any attempt at a rescue, and probably, they thought, there wouldn't be. The English spies would never be so foolish as to walk into a guard-room, just like that.

But André sat on, upright as he made out reports at a table, looking round every now and then to be certain that his men were alert and ready for action, should it prove necessary.

Then suddenly, noises outside began to penetrate the guard-room from the courtyard that fronted it, and the men lifted their heads in a surge of interest. Girls! Women! The next moment, the door was flung open, and the room seemed to be filed with frilled petticoats and chattering voices, snatches of song, and the reek of perfume and wine.

The guard who had been on duty at the gate of the courtyard tried to explain to André, who had jumped to his feet, "I couldn't keep them out, *Monsieur le Capitaine*. They said they wanted to bring comfort to the men who were doing such a wonderful job guarding our prisoners — they almost knocked me off my feet!"

André looked round him in utter exasperation, while he debated what to do. They were girls off the streets, undoubtedly, and probably they had the best of intentions, if they had wanted, as the guard said, to cheer the men during the long night. Their behaviour did not appear to be that of seeking for custom, but they were encouraging the guards to enjoy themselves, perching themselves on the men's knees, offering them jugs of wine and twining their arms round hairy necks, while they kissed weather-beaten cheeks and sang, laughing along with the men.

Then he noticed one of the girls who stood alone, a slim figure in a red gown which revealed a dainty figure, not the blowzy curves that most of the other girls possessed. Her hair, too, was shorter than theirs, a cloud of flaxen curls that framed a face that, in its delicate beauty, caught at his heart. She was not throwing herself at the guards, as the rest of the girls were doing, but was standing quietly, holding a jug of wine, waiting for someone to approach her.

André crossed the room — with some difficulty, since his way was hampered by waving feet beneath mounds of petticoats, and feminine hands that thrust wine towards him, laughing up into his face. He touched the girl on the shoulder.

She turned immediately, like a cat

ready to spring, then smiled. "Some wine, perhaps?"

Her accent was quaint, and he decided she must be from the country, and had only just joined the band of 'ladies of the night.' Certainly she did not know how to entice a man, and yet, he thought wryly, just the sight of her had brought him all the way across the room.

Trying to make himself heard above the din, he asked, "What is your name?"

"Pardon, monsieur?"

She could not hear him. He took her wrist and pulled her through into the tiny office, then shut the door so that the noise was lessened a few degrees. She seemed uneasy, and he reassured her at once.

"Do not be afraid, I won't hurt you. I am Captain André Dubois." He saw her draw in her breath quickly. "Who are you? What is your name? You're different," he said, not knowing why he should be so fascinated by a common, street girl, when titled ladies had failed to attract him.

Her long eye-lashes fell to veil her eyes, and he saw in the light of the lamp he had lit that the lashes were golden, like her hair. He had a sudden urge to touch those flaxen locks, but he resisted it. She was not like the others, he reminded himself, and he did not want to frighten her away.

Then she looked up, and he saw that her eyes were a clear, flawless green; beautiful eyes, he thought, the most beautiful eyes he had ever seen, eyes in which a man could drown.

"I am called Yvette, Monsieur le Capitaine," she answered in that quaint accent, her beautiful, green eyes upon him.

There was a sudden interruption. One of the girls — it was Scarface's woman afraid for Letty's safety — flung open the door and, swaying as though half-drunk, laughingly demanded, "Having trouble, Yvette? We came here only to cheer you men, you know, and bring some wine, and a few kisses."

Letty smiled. "I can manage, thanks, Isabeau."

"I am merely talking to this young lady," André said stiffly. "I would be obliged if you did not disturb us again. I won't lay a finger on her, I swear it."

"If you say so." Isabeau shrugged, and closed the door. She looked round the room, which was noisier than ever, then slipped out of the guard-room door. She had managed to gather from one of the men that the 'important prisoner' was in the farthest cell in the building; a fact which was extremely helpful, since any noise they made in trying to get him out was less likely to be heard.

She whistled softly in the dark of the courtyard, and a crowd of shadows gathered round.

"The farthest cell — on the corner," she whispered. "Now I'll get back to try to stir up the noise even more. We're lucky. The Captain seems to be fascinated by Letty and he's taken her into a little office to talk to her, so his attention is diverted. Good luck!"

Then she had slipped away again, while the men, who were waiting, padded on muffled shoes to the cell she had indicated.

David stood beneath the bars, trying to see something or hear movement in the darkness within.

"Greville?" he whispered in English. "Are you there?"

"*Je suis ici*," came the cautious reply.

"Friends!" David said quickly. "We're here to rescue you. Stand away from the bars. We're going to break them down and get you out."

As they all stood tensely, listening to the uproar from the guard-room, Hercule lifted his massive hands to the bars, and exerted all his mighty strength. The iron came away from the walls, and, panting heavily, he tackled the next two bars. In a very short time, the window was a gaping hole in the wall.

David whispered again, "Greville, can you climb on something and reach the window?"

"I'll try," came the response from within, and there was the sound of something being dragged along the floor as he moved his make-shift bunk, and put the bucket which stood in the corner upside-down on the top. Then, his injured leg dragging, he climed up and managed to get his head through the window, breathing in the night air in great gulps.

Hands reached to assist him and, after a great deal of squirming and wriggling, his rags torn from his body and his flesh scratched and bruised by the rough walls, he managed to slither through the gap into the arms that were waiting for him.

"Hercule, carry him on your back," Scarface commanded and the giant picked up Greville, as though he had been a toy, just before Letty's brother passed into unconsciousness. Like shadows, the group of men melted silently out of the courtyard, past the guard, who had been felled by a blow from behind, and were swallowed up in the dark alleys of Paris.

★ ★ ★

"Yvette — that is a pretty name," André said, as soon as Isabeau had shut the door. Letty clasped her ringless hands together and looked down again. She had been warned to remove her wedding ring, and David had it safely.

"Do you come from the country?" André continued, then he waved an impatient hand. "Never mind. I don't care where you come from. Do you realise that I have been chased by women for years, that none of them has interested me before — but when I saw you standing there, Yvette, something happened to me. I know what your profession is, but even that does not seem to matter. You are the one woman in the world that I want."

He hesitated as she looked at him

131

questioningly, then went on, half to himself, "Is this how it happens? That you see somebody and know that this is love? I don't know, Yvette, I have never been in love before, but I think I love you."

Letty looked up at him, and even as she seemed to be considering his words, she was wondering how the plan was going, whether Greville was safe yet. At least, though, she thought, it seemed that she had been able to help a little, by attracting the attention of the dangerous Captain and keeping him occupied. She had not intended to flirt with him, nor expected him to become interested in her, but David would understand that she must play the part of 'Yvette' for all their sakes.

She gave a shy smile. "You are very handsome, *Monsieur le Capitaine*, and a gentleman. I am — I am — I do not know what to say."

"Say you might come to love me," he pleaded, taking her hand, and she did not pull it away. "The more I look at you, the more I love you. Yvette, I promised your friend I would not hurt you, but — you tempt me so. I want to take you in my arms and hold you close to my heart, I want to kiss you."

Letty blushed.

"May I kiss you?" André asked humbly, and when she did not reply, he took her gently into his arms, as though she was a figurine that might break, and kissed her long and lingeringly on the lips.

"Oh, David! Forgive me," Letty thought, even as she allowed a shy response, and put her arms about him. She was sorry that the Captain had fallen in love with her, for how would he react when he realised she had in fact been one of the English spies, and that she had only been pretending? She had no wish to break hearts, and she could feel André's heart beating frantically against her breast. Pity for him swept over her, and she put up a tentative hand and touched his cheek.

He sank to his knees, holding her in a fierce embrace round the waist, and burying his face in her gown.

"Oh, Yvette, my little one, my darling," he murmured, overcome.

The door opened very softly at that moment, but André did not notice. Letty watched with wide eyes as Isabeau tip-toed in, her finger to her lips. The dark-haired girl lifted a paper-weight from the desk, and Letty gave a cry as Isabeau brought it down on André's head. Without a sound, he crumpled, and Letty felt her wrist seized.

"One of the girls was waiting outside, and she's come in to tell us the men have gone," Isabeau hissed. "Come on. It's time for all of us to leave, too."

Letty spared one backward glance for the slumped figure of the Captain, then she was in the guard-room where the other girls were preparing to depart with noisy kisses and good-byes to the men, who were reluctant for them to leave. Then the night air claimed the crowd of 'ladies', and the guard-room was left silent. With the candles guttering amid pools of spilt wine, and some of the men sprawled drunkenly in their chairs, only snores broke the sudden quietness, and from the little office, there was no sound at all.

★ ★ ★

Once safely back in the security of the crypt, Letty had eyes for no one but David. He had just been speaking intently to Scarface, thanking him, when she ran to him, and hid her face against his shoulder, feeling his beloved arms close round her.

"Oh, David, I had to do it," she cried. "I had to let him tell me he loved me, and I couldn't reveal that I was already married. But I did not want to hurt anyone, and I fear he will be very hurt. He was so gentle and so sincere. Oh, David, tell me I did the right thing!"

"Hush, sweet, hush, of course you

did," David assured her comfortingly, not knowing what she was talking about. But his eyes were sparkling. "Don't you want to see Greville?"

Letty wiped away the tears that had sprung to her lashes, and joy filled her face.

"Oh, yes!" she exclaimed, and David smiled as he led her to where Greville lay on one of the makeshift pallets amid the smoke and the flickering light of the candles. Letty was at his side immediately, and the two, brother and sister, hugged each other. There was no need for words.

"You're thin, Greville," she said at last. "And there is a scar on your cheek," Letty said anxiously, as they drew apart, their hands still entwined.

"Old Mother Agnes has made me more comfortable than I have been in a long while." Greville grinned. "She's a witch, I'm certain of it. A good wash and shave worked wonders, but I swear there is magic in the salve she has put on my wounds."

Wounds?" Letty, echoed, going pale. "Oh, Greville, I knew it. I had a dream on the ship and I saw you bruised and bleeding, did I not, David?"

David came forward, and Letty blushed at the question in her brother's eyes.

"Greville, may I present Mr David Gray. My husband," she said proudly.

Greville's eyes twinkled. "Husband?"

"It's a long story, but you shall hear it in good time, brother-in-law." David grinned, as the two men formally shook hands. "But do not fear, this is no pretence, Letty and I have been joined in matrimony, in church, until death shall part us. Here is your ring, my darling," he added, reaching for Sophie's mother's ring, which he had put for safe keeping on to his little finger, and Letty slid it back on to her own.

"Come now," Scarface told them, appearing at David's side. "The young gentleman requires as much rest as he can get. He is weak and needs to build up his strength for your journey. Also, Mother Agnes informs me that apart from the wounds and bruises on his body, one of his legs is broken — a clean break, fortunately. She has set it, but it will make the journey difficult for him."

"How did that happen?" Letty demanded, and Greville shrugged as best he could while lying back on his pallet. He had to admit that, though it was wonderful to be free and to see Letty again, he felt exhausted.

"A stray bullet," he said lightly. "Let's not talk of it."

"Leave him to rest. You will have time to explain everything on your journey back to the coast," Scarface said, putting his hands on David's and Letty's shoulders and drawing them away. Almost before they had turned from him, Greville had fallen into a deep sleep.

Letty looked up at the gangleader, and her eyes were moist. "How can we thank you — all of you?" she said, her voice trembling, and he gave his twisted smile.

"By escaping safely from Paris. But our plan has worked, your brother is safe, why the tears now?"

"I will never forget you, any of you," Letty choked.

David, putting an arm gently round her, said, "Come, my darling, you are overwrought. You need sleep too." But over her shoulder, as he led her to their pallets, he mouthed, 'Women!' at Scarface, and the gangleader's roar of laughter echoed round the stone arches of the crypt.

8

BY the following morning, events were moving swiftly. André Dubois had reported the escape of the important political prisoner, and a patrol was being organised to capture the three English spies. He insisted, since he had been responsible for Greville when the escape had taken place, upon leading the search personally.

"I assure you, sir, I will do my utmost to hunt them down and make certain they do not leave Paris," he assured his superior, through set lips. His heart was sore, for the memory of the green-eyed girl in his arms haunted him. It was the first time he had been in love, and he could not bear the thought of losing her.

Meanwhile, as Greville and Letty slept in the crypt, Scarface too had sent out his spies. He quietly took David to one side when Pierre le Grand returned after making an inspection of the place where Lucien was to meet them that night.

"I am afraid you will have to change your plans," the gangleader warned. "Pierre reports that the river is being watched, and he has sent a secret message to Lucien to make no contact with you. Anyone who does will be arrested as a traitor. You must delay your escape no longer. Soldiers are everywhere. It is imperative that you leave Paris at once."

David's face grew anxious as he glanced in the direction of the sleeping Letty. "But how?" he asked.

Scarface gave his twisted smile. "He who dares, wins," he replied. "We will help you as much as we can but after you leave Paris, you have the journey to the coast, and you will need a guide. I have summoned a man here to meet you. He is an adventurer, a soldier-of-fortune. He will, I hope, undertake to guide you to where your ship is waiting. But he will require to be paid."

"How much?" David asked, through dry lips, and Scarface waved a careless hand.

"Give him ten gold pieces, no more. Have it ready when he comes. And we shall need another gold piece for some of my men to buy a cart and a horse for you to ride."

"You mean, we are just going to ride out of Paris in daylight?" David queried in amazement.

Pierre cackled. "Just so. But Luc will be with you once you have left the city, until then, you have us on your side, so how can you lose?"

"You had better rouse madame, and the young man, and warn them to prepare to leave as quickly as possible," Scarface told David. "The cart is for madame and her bother. Luc will drive it, and you will ride alongside. But everything you need to take with you must be in that cart, for there will be no turning back."

★ ★ ★

The guard who had been posted at a gate out of the city was called Jean, and he flattered himself that he had a way with women. Certainly he was not taking his task, which was to watch for three English spies, very seriously, for this small gateway was unimportant, he thought. He was far more interested in the pretty girl with the long, black hair who was lingering enticingly not far away, than in the country people who were the only ones to pass in and out.

Desultorily, he checked each passer-by, but his mind was on the girl, who at length came across and gave him a languishing smile. They were soon deep in conversation, and though he continued to scan the people who passed through the gate, and question them briefly about their business, his brain was already racing ahead to the evening, when Marie, for that, she told him, was her name, had promised to meet him.

143

A cart came rumbling towards the gate, with a man riding beside it, and Jean looked up, annoyed at being interrupted.

"Your business?" he demanded.

The driver of the cart, a hard-featured man who looked like some sort of gipsy, with a gold ring in one ear, gestured over his shoulder. "My brother is ill. We're taking him to his parents in Compiegne. That's his sister tending him — my sister, too, of course. Mind you, between you and me, I don't think he'll make the journey."

"Why not?" Jean demanded, staring into the cart, where a young man lay on a makeshift bed of rags and blankets, with a fair-haired girl, in a red peasant dress, kneeling beside him, wiping his forehead solicitously. She looked up at the driver, and spoke with a tremor in her voice.

"Don't say that, Giles! Mother and Father will know what to do."

"If they're still there. Perhaps the fair

144

has moved on," the rider of the horse interrupted, stifling a yawn. He gave Jean a hard stare, and said, "I wouldn't venture too close to him, if I were you. Celine insists that it's only a fever, but I've seen the spots. The plague . . . "

"Plague?"

Jean went pale and stepped hastily back from the cart. "Go on, get on your way," he snapped, waving them through the gate, and the cart passed him by. As it did so, he crossed himself, and stood watching it until it disappeared round a clump of trees. Then he turned back to Marie. But to his frustration and dismay, she had gone, with not a word of good-bye; and somehow, he didn't think she would keep her promise to meet him that evening.

★ ★ ★

André snapped his whip against his polished boots, and repeated incredulously, "You actually let them through?

When you knew we were searching for two men and a woman — one a man who can't walk very well? And that the woman has fair hair?"

Poor Jean hardly dared to raise his eyes. He stared at the ground, his face scarlet, as he stammered; "*Pardon, Monsieur le Capitaine*. But they said the man in the cart had the plague."

The Captain sighed. "I suppose I can't blame you too much. But where did they go? Which way?"

"They said they were going to Compiegne, *Monsieur le Capitaine*," Jean answered eagerly, glad to be able to say something right after his dreadful blunder.

André shook his head. "Compiegne? Never. We'll take the road to Beauvais. He swung himself back into the saddle of his horse, and waved his men on. The patrol clattered out beneath the arch of the gate, and galloped off.

From their hiding-place in a thicket half a mile away, Letty, David, Greville and Luc, their guide, watched them go, and Luc gave a satisfied smile.

"As I thought. They have taken the other road. They will imagine we are heading for Calais." He drew a rough map on the dirt patch in front of them, with a stick. "What we do is to head west, as they go north. It will take a long time to occur to them that we are going right across France to Brest, instead of making for the nearest part of the coast. We should have gained enough time to be able to get to Brest long before they catch up with us. If they ever do." He climbed back on to the cart, and whipped up the horse in the shafts, clicking his tongue to her. The cart pulled out of the trees, and with David riding beside them, they jolted off down the opposite road from André and his men . . .

As they travelled, Letty could not help constantly staring back in the direction they had come, half-expecting to see the uniforms of the Captain and his patrol closing in on them. Yet the country roads along which Luc took them were peaceful and empty in the mellow sunlight.

Her other concern was Greville, who was jolted and bounced about on the boards of the cart so that by the time they stopped in the evening, his wounds were sore, his leg aching badly, and his back stiff.

"Never mind me, little sister," he told Letty, trying to make light of it. "I can take it. And, what's more, I will have accomplished my mission if we reach the Columbella safely," he told her proudly. "I have all the information I was sent to obtain, here in my head, memorised."

Letty ran a distracted hand through her hair. "Oh, of course, I had forgotten that you were on a secret mission," she replied. "So much has happened that now, my only thought is for us all to escape."

They were sitting in a great barn, on a pile of hay. Luc had spun the farmer a tale that they were wandering gipsies, one of whom had met with an accident, and obtained permission, assisted by the surreptitious clink of a coin into the man's hand, for them to spend the night resting in the barn. The same coin had also purchased them food and drink, and care for their two horses.

While they ate the bread and cheese and fruit that had been brought to them by the farmer, Letty and David between them told Greville all that had happened since they last met, and he was sincere in his congratulations on their marriage.

Luc, who was sitting near the barn door, watching the stars, reminded them that they would need to be on their way early in the morning, and reluctantly, for it was so wonderful to be together again, David, Letty and Greville, finished off the milk that had been part of their meal, and settled down to sleep in the straw, wrapped in their blankets.

The morning came all to soon, Letty thought, as she tidied herself and splashed her face at the pump in the farm yard. Though, each day now was one day nearer to safety, and a peaceful life in England with her beloved David.

She washed Greville as best she could, and assisted him to his bed in the cart, while Luc, who had been up and about long before the others, sat in the driving seat, idly flicking the reins. David's horse was led out, ready saddled by the farmer, and David put his foot in the stirrup. They were on their way in a few moments, after thanking the farmer and saying goodbye.

The farmer stood in the fresh morning, with the rising sun casting long shadows about him, and watched the cart until it was out of sight. In his hand, he carefully weighed the coin Luc had given him, and his face had taken on a foxy look. Then, as though he had made up his mind, he went briskly indoors, spoke briefly to his wife, and went out to saddle one of his own horses. He turned the mare's head in the direction of Paris, and the authorities.

He would tell them how he'd overheard his visitors speaking in English and talking of escape by ship. And he was sure to be handsomely rewarded for the information.

★ ★ ★

So the next night, while the fugitives slept as best they could in the cart, hidden among some trees, with food that Luc had procured from a village they had passed through — for he felt in his bones that it would be safer from now on to avoid trying to seek shelter in barns and farms — a messenger from Paris rode swiftly through the night in the direction of Beauvais. He passed the town, for André and his men had ridden fast and furiously, and at length, as the morning was breaking, located the Captain and his patrol lodging in the inn of a small village.

When he relayed his message, André

almost exploded. "We have lost two days, do you realise that?" he demanded. "They have two days' start on us now — even if we knew where they were going!"

"I am sorry, *Monsieur le Capitaine*," the messenger stammered. He was almost dropping with fatigue. "I was merely doing my duty."

The young captain noticed his state for the first time. "Yes, of course. You have done well. You may rest now, before you return to Paris, but my men and I will set out immediately. No wonder we could find no trace of them!"

He hurried his men into action like a maniac, for always, now, in his head, was the thought of his love, the girl with the green eyes. She had begun to haunt him, like some siren of old, who lured sailors to destruction on the rocks with their ships. The small, delicate face, the cloud of pale hair, and the feel of her lips beneath his own, his memories beat in his head with every beat of his horse's hooves, and he urged his men to go faster, so that they wondered at his urgency.

And though André knew his love was an English spy, it made no difference to his feelings. He wanted her, he wanted to find her, to plead his love yet again, to beg her on his knees never to leave him, for there would never be any other woman who could take the place she had taken in his heart.

9

THE days had become monotonous for the fugitives. Luc too drove them as fast as he dared, using short cuts and pathways that bounced the cart so that Greville bit his lip to save himself crying out against the pain in his leg, and Letty was almost thrown from her place beside him.

All the long days, from dawn until it was too dark for them to see their way, Luc pushed relentlessly on towards the coast, stopping only at small villages to buy food and drink, and see to the needs of the horses. At nights, they huddled together beneath their blankets, and snatched what sleep they could, before Luc urged them on again.

Letty began to feel that the journey had gone on for ever, but still, to her great relief, there was no sign of André and his men, and one day, Luc announced that they were only a short distance now from the place where Columbella would be awaiting them.

"We have been lucky," he said, and gave a crooked smile. "And I have some good news for you. Tonight you can sleep in comfort. There is a gipsy encampment not far away, and I think we can relax enough to stay there for the night. They are true Romanies, and I know them. They will be only too pleased to welcome you, for the Romanies are a law unto themselves, and they will not care whether you are English or French."

It was almost with a feeling of holiday that they arrived at the gipsy encampment, and Luc quickly explained the situation to the Gipsy Chief, who told the bedraggled travellers, with immense dignity, that they were welcome to stay for as long as they wished.

"One night only," Luc decreed.

"Then we must be on our way. Two more days should bring us to the coast."

But it was with excitement that David and Letty indulged in the luxury of hot water to wash for the first time in many days, and for the men to shave off the stubble that had grown during their mad ride. Greville was given a soft bed, and one of the gipsy women tended his wounds, and put healing salve on his bruises. His broken leg was healing well, she assured him, but it would take a long time before he could walk on it properly again, and she re-set it in splints for the bone to continue to heal.

Then, as evening and the soft country twilight was drawing in, they sat with the Romanies for a meal that seemed to them all to be the most delicious they had ever tasted. The Gipsy Chief smiled as he told them that in their honour, there would be dancing and music afterwards, and Letty and David held hands like any young couple newly wed, their hearts light.

While they were eating, however, a rider came dashing into the centre of the encampment, and spoke hurriedly to the Chief, who came over to the fugitives at once.

"You are in danger. One of the men who keeps a watch for us tells me that a patrol is not far away, and they are heading directly for the camp."

"It must be the Captain and his men, they have caught up with us at last," Letty cried in distress. "Where can we hide? What shall we do?"

"The young men with the broken leg, some of our men will carry him into the forest, for he cannot be disguised, and they will search every wagon," the Chief said quickly, and beckoned to three burly gipsies, who disappeared in the gathering darkness, carrying Greville with them on a make-shift stretcher.

"Now, we will carry on the dancing as planned, and tell the Captain we are celebrating a wedding." He looked at Letty. "Your gown — have you another?" And, as Letty shook her head, he ordered one of the girls to take her and give her a different one to wear.

"And her hair must be covered," he ordered. "She will be recognised by her hair. In fact, I have it, we will pretend that you two are the ones who are being wed, and then she can cover her head with a veil, so that her face is not visible." Then he turned to David, saying, "You, too, can wear festive clothes, and we will parade you both before the Captain's very eyes. We must be daring; do you think you have the courage to carry it off?"

"We can do anything you ask," David promised recklessly, and the scene was quickly arranged, with Letty, her head covered with a veil heavily embroidered with sequins, sitting by David in the centre of the camp. The rest of the gipsies in their colourful costumes danced and sang in a circle about them. Letty wore her wedding ring, and sat with her hands folded in her lap, trying to look like a happy young bride, though inwardly, she was trembling.

The scene had hardly been arranged, and the wine passed round, when André and his men galloped without ceremony into the centre of the encampment, where the gipsies had lit a great fire, and were dancing and singing in a circle around it.

"Stop! Stop the music! Stop the dancing!" shouted André, sliding from his horse, and the Gipsy Chief stood up and came forward to him.

"Sir, have some respect for our customs," he said with dignified outrage. "We are holding a wedding feast."

"Search the wagons!" André ordered his men, and they scattered to obey his command.

The Chief continued to protest, "At least tell us what you are looking for. We are Romanies, we have no secrets from the police."

"Three people — no, four, with their French accomplice. They are travelling in a cart, with one of them riding a horse. One of them has a broken leg. We know they came this way, we checked at the last village, and they were seen," André snapped. "They are English spies."

The gipsies were clustering round, as though bewildered, and the Chief spoke with a shrug. "We have horses, we have carts. But these people you speak of — "

"Monsieur le Capitaine!" came an excited cry, and one of the men from the patrol came out of a wagon, holding Letty's crumped red gown in his hand. "This is her gown. Pushed down behind some bedding."

"Then they are here!" André's cry was a shout of triumph. He seized the Chief by the shoulder, and shook him. "Where is she? Where? Tell me, or by God we will take this camp apart and arrest the lot of you!"

The Chief pulled himself free and

drew himself up majestically. "I was just about to tell you what we know," he said, with no trace of fear, although the discovery of Letty's gown had shaken him. It was something they had overlooked. He thought quickly, took a deep breath, and continued; "They passed us earlier on today, and stopped to ask for food and water. We did not know who they were, but a wedding is a wedding, and we offered them our hospitality and asked them to stay for the festivities."

André's gaze was darting everywhere in the light of the fire, and he looked at the young couple sitting holding hands in the centre of the circle. The girl lifted her hand to her cheek, as though she was crying, and the firelight glittered on the wide gold band she was wearing. André looked away, and back at the Chief.

"Well?" he demanded.

The Chief shrugged. "They would not stay. They said they were in too much of a hurry, and they drove off," he said. "They told us they were heading for the coast, that they were going south." He pointed into the darkness. "We saw them leave along that very road."

"And the girl's gown?" André demanded. His voice was shaking. He could picture her wearing it, the way she had stood in the guard-room, the way it had hung on her slender figure. "Why is it hidden in one of your vans?"

"Hidden? It is not hidden, or your men would not have found it," the Chief countered, with spirit. "The young woman told us her gown was torn, and asked if she could purchase another from us. We gave her — I think it was a blue one. No, it was one of Regine's, green to match her eyes."

"Yes, her eyes are green," André muttered. He held out a hand. "I will take the gown." Silently, it was handed to him, and he folded it gently away as though it was very precious to him.

From beneath her veil, where she

was trying not to shake with nerves, Letty saw the gesture, and bit her lip. So he really loved her. Tears started to her eyes at the heart-break she had so unwittingly caused, and it was only the pressure of David's fingers on her own that saved her from breaking down.

Then André gave a last look round the camp. "Which road? Tell me again," he said, and the Chief pointed.

"I heard them say they might stop for a rest past the next village, but the Frenchman argued with them to carry on moving. So where you will find them, I do not know." he shrugged.

"Thank you. I apologise for disturbing your wedding festivities," André said, with a formal bow. He turned to David and Letty, and the girl's heart gave a lurch of panic. But all André said, in a tone which brought the tears to her eyes again, was, "May I wish every health and happiness to the bride and groom."

Then the patrol was gone, and the sounds of their horses faded into the

163

distance. The Chief gave a signal, and the gipsies began their music and dancing once more. But Letty was wiping her eyes beneath the veil that had saved her.

"Oh, David! He really does love me," she choked. "I did not want him to love me — but for him to wish me health and happiness with another man, when his own heart's desire will never be fulfilled — I cannot bear it. Oh, David, let us get away, back to England, as soon as we can," Letty cried.

Just then the Chief beckoned to them. "Change back into your own clothes — we will indeed give you another gown, lady — and I will have them prepare your cart and horses as soon as possible. There is moonlight tonight, and it will take you only another night and a day to reach the coast, if you set off now. I will send a guide with you, who knows these paths as he knows the lines upon his hand.

"I have sent the patrol in the opposite

direction, but maybe in the morning, maybe later, they will turn back. By then, we must all be gone, or their wrath will fall upon my people. We will find a new home. Hurry, the dancing is over now, and there is danger for us all, until we get safely away."

Letty and David, as well as the gipsies, ran immediately to carry out his bidding, fear at their heels, and within half an hour, the fugitives had set of with their gipsy guide in the silver moonlight, while the camp was hastily being packed up.

An hour later, all trace of the encampment itself had disappeared.

★ ★ ★

With their gipsy guide sitting beside Luc on the driving seat, the cart rumbled on through the night, the moonlight lighting up the countryside so that it was almost as bright as day. Greville and Letty clung to the sides, and David rode swiftly along behind them on his horse, occasionally looking back for signs of pursuit.

None of them slept, and Letty did not think she would ever be able to sleep again for anxiety and fear. The knowledge that André and his patrol might turn back at any moment and catch up with the cart made every breath she took rasp in her throat with panic.

"Can't we go faster?" she cried to Luc.

"I am going as fast as the cart will take us, he said, over his shoulder.

On, on through the night and, to Letty's dazed surprise, the dawn came at last, and it was day. That was when it happened. The cart jolted over a stone, and there was a loud splintering.

She screamed as she was thrown headlong into some long grass, and Greville let out a cry of pain as the cart tipped and he too slid over the side, grasping frantically at the wooden boards to save a fall on to the path. He hung there, half in and half out, until David came quickly to his assistance.

Letty was stunned for a few moments, then she lifted her head, realised that nothing was broken, and struggled to sit up. David, who was supporting Greville, looked round at her.

"Are you all right, my darling?"

"I think so. But what happened?" she asked, raising a dazed hand to her head. Luc and the gipsy were inspecting the wheel that had come off the cart.

"Disaster," Luc told her, "for the cart has broken down, and we have no tools, nor the time, to repair it. But we are still a day's journey from Brest. We cannot walk, as you would not get there in time to give your ship its signal."

They looked at each other in the early morning sunshine, dismay on their faces.

"What can we do? Can't we buy another cart?" David asked grimly, and Luc waved a hand round at the deserted countryside.

"From where?" he asked.

Greville was panting after his fall, but his eyes were resolute.

"It is I who am hindering you. Leave me, and go on with the horses," he said to Letty. She gave a cry of anguish and ran to throw her arms around him. "Never, never, Greville. David and I have not come all this way to rescue you only to leave you here for the authorities to find again."

Luc and the gipsy conferring in quick French, with many gestures.

After some moments, they turned to the fugitives, and Luc spoke grimly. "There is only one thing to be done. Fortunately, the horses are good, strong beasts, though they are tired, for, like us, they have had no sleep last night. But I know the exact place where you are to meet up with your ship, and I weigh less than Jerome here, so we have decided that he will leave us, and we four will go on, two on each horse.

"We will not be able to go very quickly, but by using paths Jerome has just described to me, we should be in time for you to signal for rescue tonight."

"What about Greville?" Letty demanded at once, her arm about her brother.

Luc shrugged. "He will have to manage as best he can. You and he are the lightest of us. If we're to split our weight evenly between the horses, you will ride with your husband, and your brother will come with me."

"But that's impossible — " Letty began in distress.

Greville laid a quick finger across her lips. "I'll manage somehow," he told Luc, and the soldier-of-fortune nodded, approving the young man's courage.

"First we must hide the cart, though it would be better if we were to leave Jerome to do that, and get on our way," he declared. "Leave everything that isn't absolutely necessary behind — the blankets, everything. We must

169

not burden the beasts any more than we need to."

So, leaving coats,blankets, everything except the barest minimum of clothing and David's money-belt, David and Letty scrambled on to one of the horses, with Letty insisting on riding astride and tucking up her petticoats, so that she could cling to David's waist.

They waited, while Luc mounted the other horse, and Greville was assisted by the burly Jerome to clamber awkwardly astride behind their guide. His broken leg hung uselessly in its splints, and his face paled at the pain, but he set his mouth grimly.

He seized Luc round the waits, and muttered to him, "I shall have to hold very tightly, I'm afraid, or I may fall. I'll try not to be a greater nuisance than I can help."

"You are a young man of great courage, *mon ami*," Luc told him.

Greville lowered his voice even more.

"Don't tell my sister I am in pain. I can stand it. I hope I won't pass out, that's all."

"I will ride as carefully as I can," Luc assured him, and he called to David. "You are ready? Then *en avant*. We must reach the coast tonight."

With quick good-byes to Jerome, they rode off, and only Luc knew of Greville's involuntary moan as the motion of the horse jolted his leg.

So the beasts, with their double burdens, disappeared along a pathway into trees, where the sunlight dappled them with shade, through the leaves.

Jerome, left standing alone beside the wrecked cart, dragged it, as best he could, to be hidden by some bushes; and threw everything after it, including the wheel that had fallen off. He looked round. The only signs of what had happened were some scruffling in the dust of the road, and Jerome took a branch from a tree, and smoothed the marks out. Then, satisfied that he had done everything he could to assist the fugitives, he set off at an easy stride in a direction which would lead him to the road the rest of the gipsies had decided to take in their flight from the encampment.

10

THE sun rose in a clear sky, and the day grew hotter and hotter. Letty's throat was parched, but she proudly refused to be the first to ask Luc to stop so that she could drink. It was only when Greville suddenly slid from his horse's back and lay unconscious in the roadway that Luc drew rein, and David did the same. Letty ran to her brother.

"Water. We must have water," she cried desperately.

Luc looked round the forest on one side, and the fields on the other. He spotted the cottage some distance away, and said abruptly, "I'll fetch some. We must have water for the horses too, so I'll take them with me, and try to get us something to eat."

At the mention of food, Letty's stomach heaved, since they had eaten nothing since the meal with gipsies the previous night, but she was far more concerned about Greville.

With David's help, she straightened his splinted leg, glad he could not feel the pain, and tried to make him comfortable with his head cradled in her lap. After a few moments, his eyes fluttered open.

"Water!" he croaked.

Letty stroked the perspiration from his forehead and smoothed back his hair. "Luc has gone to get some. Oh, Greville, you should have stopped us before this if you were feeling so ill."

"No time — " Greville managed to gasp, then lay there weakly, while David and Letty waited, their gazes strained on the cottage where Luc had disappeared with the horses, who were weary by now, and stumbling.

They were glad of the shade of the tree beneath which they were sitting, but even as they waited, Letty's eyes moved fearfully back down the road they had travelled, terrified lest she should see the sun glittering on the uniforms of André and his men.

After only a short time, Luc came across the fields towards them, followed by a middle-aged woman who reminded Letty of Sophie, in her bonnet and apron. Luc was carrying a pail and mug, and the woman held up her apron, which obviously contained food.

"This good lady has kindly given us water, and something to eat," Luc said briefly. They all drank thirstily, Letty making sure that Greville's thirst was satisfied, and that a little water was spared to splash his face and neck, and cool his hot brow.

"*Alors*," the countrywoman cried. "The poor young man! You did not tell me he was ill! he should be resting in a soft bed in his condition, not gadding about the country." And she glared at Luc, as though he had insulted her. "Bring him to the cottage at once, and I will nurse him. Making him ride a horse, indeed, with a leg that anyone can see is broken!"

The fugitives looked at each other. "Madame, you are very kind, but we must get to the coast tonight," Luc told her, with a slight bow.

"But he needs rest — just a little rest, Luc," Letty pleaded.

The countrywomen was regarding them, hands on hips, and she put in suspiciously, "Now then, now then, what is all this? Your horses, poor beasts, are almost dead on their feet, you have a young man here who is almost dead from fatigue, and — "

Letty went across and took the good woman's hand. "Madame," she said in her quaint French. "You are kind, you are good, you will not betray us. We are English, and tonight we must reach the coast, and safety, for there is a patrol seeking us, and it may be only a mile or two behind us.

"We have done nothing wrong, I swear, only rescued my brother, who as you can see, has been beaten up by the authorities as an English prisoner." Tears were beginning to trickle down from her green eyes, and the woman put a comforting arm round her trembling shoulders.

"You all need rest," she declared firmly, and added, glaring at Luc, "even you. Will an hour matter so much? You can make the coast easily before dark, you have only a few miles left. Come to the cottage for an hour, and at least let me see to this young man's leg. As for the patrol — pah!" And she spat unceremoniously into the road, a dangerous glitter in her eyes. "I will deal with them. Anyone can see you are no danger to France — a sweet, angel girl, and such upright young men."

She glared at Luc again. "You're the only one who looks like a scoundrel to me, and you're as French as they come. Bring them with you, at once, and my brother and I will sort you out."

She turned on her heel, and set off without looking back, and Luc, shrugging, helped Greville to his feet, and, with the assistance of David and

Letty, half-carried him across the fields to the little cottage, which proved to be a small-holding, with chickens and geese, and stables surrounding it.

"If the patrol should come, you will be safer in the stables," the countrywoman told them. "You can hide in the straw. And my brother, just for the sake of safety, you understand, will take your horses up to our top field, where the police will not see them, mingled with our own. He has fed and watered the beasts, and there they can rest. Now, let me see to the young man."

The fugitives sank into the straw in the stables, and Grevile was lowered gently on to the pile of blankets that had been brought to give him something comfortable to lie on. The woman bustled back and forth, telling them her name was Francine, and her brother, Francois. She was quite obviously the one in charge of the family's affairs, and her tall, hulking brother said nothing, but simply did as she bid him; while she chattered on as she tended to Greville's wounds, made him comfortable, and gave him some food.

The she turned to the others. "Come now, into the kitchen with you for a meal. When did you last eat?" she demanded, and ushered them to sit round a rough table, where steaming soup and fresh bread were placed before them, together with glasses of home-made wine.

They all ate eagerly, but Letty ventured to ask, "What if the police should come? How will we know?"

Francois is keeping watch," Francine assured her comfortably, and Letty allowed herself to relax a little.

After they had eaten, and were feeling distinctly better, Francine continued her organising of what they were to do, bandying words with Luc, who grinned as she called him 'scoundrel' and 'rogue.'

"Now you are all to have two hours sleep," Francine commanded. "I think if you could sleep in the hay loft, you would be safer, Francois will keep watch for you, never fear. And then we will see you safely on your journey." She clucked her tongue. "Anyone can see you have a man in charge of you, instead of a woman. A woman would have made sure you had food and rest, and not driven you to the point of exhaustion.

★ ★ ★

The fugitives had not slept for more than about half an hour, however, when Francois came hurrying into the farm kitchen and spoke to his sister. She ran into the stables, her apron flapping in the breeze.

"Quickly! Quickly! Francois has seen the patrol. It is coming over the hill, and is sure to call here. You must all hide in the hay and straw, the young man, too, and the blankets must be hidden in the house." She clapped her hands with urgency. "Burrow into the hay. I will make sure you cannot be seen and then take the blankets away.

"The young man — " she turned to Greville, who was struggling to get up, "Francois will assist you to a far corner, and we will cover you with a pile of saddles and reins. It is very dark. if we spread a little straw around, I do not think they will search an ordinary stable. Behind the manger, there, Francois."

Panic surged through the place as the blankets were hastily gathered together and, in the loft, David, Letty and Luc burrowed deep into the hay until Francine was certain that no sign of them could be seen. Greville lay in a shadowy corner with various pieces of harness and equipment piled on the dark cloth Francois had spread over his body to cover his bright hair and any sight of his face or hands.

"Let us pray none of us sneezes," David muttered to Luc.

Then, just as Francine had predicted, there sounds of hooves and jingling

181

harnesses in the yard, and André's voice could be heard through the open stable door.

"Hey! You there!"

Francine had disappeared into the house, and Francois was pretending to groom one of his own horses in the yard. The fugitives heard his slow reply.

"Yes, Monsieur le Capitaine? What can I do for you?"

Then there were quick clicks from Francine's sabots on the cobled yard, and her penetrating cry, "What do you mean by bringing your men into our yard with out so much as a 'how do you do'? Captain you may be, but we have the hens and the geese upset now, and if you put the hens off laying — "

André interrupted this outburst as patiently as he could. The little group frozen in the stables could picture the scene, with the good woman, the epitome of innocence, her hands on her hips, and the tall Captain trying to placate her.

"*Pardon, madame*, I did not mean to harm any of your property. But our mission is urgent. We are seeking three English spies and their French guide. One of the men has a broken leg, but we found the remains of their cart, in which he was travelling, farther up the road, and we know they are heading for the coast. They must be riding two horses. One of them — " his voice shook for a moment, "one of them is a girl — young, pretty, with fair hair and green eyes. Have you seen them?"

"Where did you say you found their cart?" Francine questioned, and when the Captain named the place, she gave a snort of contempt.

"That is miles away. When did you find it?"

"A few hours ago. We were sent off on a false trail by some rascally gipsies, who have since disappeared — very wisely, for if I could get my hands on them, I would force the truth from them," André said, and Letty felt a chill creep up her spine at the coldness in his voice.

Francine, however, was unmoved. "Do you mean to say that a man with a broken leg could have ridden this far in these few hours?" she cried, and gave a loud laugh. "Why, such a thing would have been impossible. No, my good Captain, you are letting your enthusiasm run away with you. Very probably these spies you are seeking hid and let you go past, or else they have gone in another direction."

"This is the quickest way to the coast," André snapped, but there was doubt in his words.

"Well, if you think they are here, you are welcome to search, so long as you do not go upsetting my chickens and making the geese nervous. But I can tell you, to save you wasting your time, that my brother and I have seen nothing of your spies," she declared. Then with finality she added, "now I am going back to the kitchen. I have the stew to season, and my bread to do, I can't spare the time to stand here talking about some mythical spies. Spies, indeed!" And with another snort, she clattered back in the direction of the house.

There was a pause, while the fugitives held their breaths. Then André spoke again, this time to Francois.

"And you, monsieur? You have seen nothing? No strangers passing along the coast path?"

Francois was a man of few words. "No," he said simply, and Letty heard André sigh with frustration.

"They have not reached this point in the path yet, obviously. Perhaps we misjudged their haste, as this good woman has suggested. Perhaps they are taking it in slow stages, and playing a game of hide-and-seek with us. He looked round. The small-holding was peaceful and innocent in the bright sunlight.

"Come," he said, and something in his voice brought a lump to Letty's throat. "We'll go back to where we found the wagon, and start again from there. We may find traces we missed."

"Our horses are tired, *Monsieur le Capitaine*," one of his men said. Another added, "They cannot go much farther."

"Then when we get back to the cart, we will rest and we will stop for food and drink for ourselves — and see to the horses' requirements," André decided.

Then as he remounted, André muttered desperately, "I must find her. Something tells me she is near but I have a feeling that, soon, it will be too late." He raised his voice and commanded the patrol forward.

"A reprieve!" David was saying joyfully. "We should gain the coast by the time they go to the remains of the cart and back. Am I not right, Luc?"

"Indeed, thanks to our good friends," Luc told him, his eyes glittering, "But whatever Francine says, we must sleep no more. We want to be ready when darkness falls — and we must not forget a lantern for your signal."

Francois was uncovering Greville and, in a fever of excitement, the others came scrambling down the ladder from the loft.

Letty went and hugged her brother. "Are you all right?" she demanded.

He nodded. "Rested and recovered. So, onward! To the coast — and to the Columbella and safety, little sister. In a few hours, all this danger and hardship will seem but a dream — it will all be over!"

Provided with three fresh horses by Francine and Francois, whom they thanked with genuine warmth — and, David insisted, with some gold pieces he pressed upon them — the little party set off.

Revived by the food they had eaten, and the rest they had had, brief though it had been, they sped through the afternoon towards the coast.

Suddenly, Letty gave a cry. "The sea! The sea!"

"We will reach your place of appointment with your ship a few miles up the coast," Luc cried to David.

"Are you certain the Columbella will be there, David?" Greville asked above the sound of their horses' hooves.

"Almost certain," David replied, with a conviction he did not quite feel. He had told the Rear-Admiral to expect them in about two weeks, and they were two days late. Would Sir Charles have waited, or would he have given up hope for them? He could only pray that Sir Charles was a patient man, prepared to give them a few days grace.

The day was drawing to a close, and the twilight was stealing in soft, blue light over the sparkling sea that was to be their salvation, when Luc stopped suddenly, drawing rein so that his mount reared.

"One moment," Luc told the others, who had also drawn rein. Then, trying not to disturb Greville, who was riding behind him, he slid from his horse's back, and lay with his ear to the ground. When he looked up, his face was sombre.

"I could sense it. I can hear them, not very far behind us, and galloping like the wind," he told the fugitives. Quickly, leave your horses and let them run away. Down there, this is the place where your ship will be awaiting you, when it is fully dark."

Letty gazed out anxiously over the darkening sea. "I cannot see any sign of a ship," she cried, and turned to David. "Oh, David, will it come?"

"As soon as dark has fallen, my darling," David reassured her, his arm round her shoulders. "But now, we must find a place to hide, before the patrol comes."

"Make your way to the water's edge, as near as you can, and pray. Pray as you have never prayed before," Luc told them. With a swift good-bye and their thanks, he was off, driving the other two horses with him, while

David and Letty assisted Greville over the stones and rocks to the edge of the cliff.

"We must climb down," David whispered, clinging to Greville's arm in case the other man fell, for he had stumbled several times. "Do you think you can do it, Greville."

"I'll do it," Greville promised, through set teeth, and, ignoring the pain in his leg, he began to descend cautiously, while the others helped him all they could, trying to keep their footing on the rocks.

They had almost reached the bottom of the cliff, and it was very nearly dark, when Letty's quick ears caught a sound, and she whispered to the others, "Ssh!"

They froze. From the top of the cliff, the sound of horses trotting came down to them, and André's voice, "Somewhere along here. Where's the light?"

A lantern flashed and another voice said, "They stopped here, but then went on. Look, here are the hoofprints in the grass."

"On, then. I must find her — I must," André cried, a note of desperation in his voice, and the patrol continued along the top of the cliff, their voices fading into the night.

"Let's pray they do not return until the Columbella has picked us up," Greville whispered and, when they were certain the patrol was out of earshot, the three stumbled the rest of the way to where the waves lapped on the shore.

They huddled together in the shelter of an overhang, and David, straining his eyes, uttered suddenly, "The Columbella! I think I see her, Quick — the signal, Greville!"

One, twice, three times, Greville, half-lying on the rocks, flashed his secret signal to Sir Charles, and tensely, they all waited.

Was that the sound of oars in rowlocks? Then, from above came the noise they most dreaded — the sound

191

of the patrol returning.

"There is a ship out there, *Monsieur le Capitaine!*" cried a voice.

André's shout rang through the night. "Then they are down there, by the sea. What are you waiting for? Take the lantern, Bring her to me, bring her to me I say! Never mind the others, but don't let her go!"

"Oh, God!" Letty prayed, clinging to David's arm, as they heard the patrol dismount and begin to clamber noisily down the cliff, lanterns lighting their way.

"There they are!" one of the men yelled, seeing the little group huddled at the water's edge, and David shut his eyes. So, they had gambled and lost! This was the end!

But even as his heart sank, Greville pulled at his arm frantically.

"Here's the boat. Quick, you'll have to help me. Into the water so that the men can pull off."

There was a whistle and, without thought, David and Letty with Greville between them, plunged waist-deep into the water, laughing for joy as the men from the Columbella dragged them over the side of the boat, and the oars pulled them from the very grasp of their would-be captors. Just too late to catch them, the patrol stood helplessly on the shore, as the fugitives were rowed swiftly into the dark, and safety.

On the cliff-top, sitting astride his horse, his cloak stirred in the cool night wind, André watched as the light from the lanterns his men held lingered on a small head of flaxen hair in the security of the boat as it disappeared into the darkness, and then vanished.

"Yvette, my love. My lost, little love," he murmurd, stricken to the soul, and he turned his horse so that before his men returned, he could wipe away the unmanly tears that had come unbidden to his eyes.

★ ★ ★

Laughing and hugging each other, Letty and David stood on the deck of the Columbella, while Sir Charles tried to gain from them a coherent story of what had occurred.

"We will tell you tomorrow, sir," David told him. "But tonight, we are so thankful to be here that I fear we are slightly delirious."

"Commander Fanshawe, I have to congratulate you on a successful mission," Sir Charles said to Greville, who was being cared for by the ship's physician as he lay on the deck, exhausted, but triumphant. "I will send your report immediately to the Admiralty."

"I owe everything to my sister and my brother-in-law, sir," Greville said.

Sir Charles blinked. "Brother-in-law? Mr Gray? Miss Fanshawe?"

"Not Miss Fanshaw any longer, sir." Letty laughed. "When I can wash and change into more suitable attire, I am going to reappear in my proper role as Mrs Gray." She took David's arm, and gazed adoringly at him. "I shall tell Papa that I greatly enjoyed my sojourn in London, and that I met the most charming gentleman, and married him."

"What shall you tell Miss Drew, who feared you might come to harm in the wicked metropolis?" Greville laughed.

Letty lowerd her lashes, and stifled a yawn. "Why, that I came to no harm at all. I think that is all anyone need to know about my visit to London," she said primly, as befitted the 'Young Lady from the Big House,' who had seen nothing, done nothing, and been nowhere. But the knowledge and suffering and pain and passion in her eyes as she turned to David, told another story.

WITH SOMEBODY ELSE
Theresa Charles

Rosamond sets off for Cornwall with Hugo to meet his family, blissfully unaware of the shocks in store for her.

A SUMMER FOR STRANGERS
Claire Hamilton

Because she had lost her job, her flat and she had no money, Tabitha agreed to pose as Adam's future wife although she believed the scheme to be deceitful and cruel.

VILLA OF SINGING WATER
Angela Petron

The disquieting incidents that occurred at the Vatican and the Colosseum did not trouble Jan at first, but then they became increasingly unpleasant and alarming.

DOCTOR NAPIER'S NURSE
Pauline Ash

When cousins Midge and Derry are entered as probationer nurses on the same day but at different hospitals they agree to exchange identities.

A GIRL LIKE JULIE
Louise Ellis

Caroline absolutely adored Hugh Barrington, but then Julie Crane came into their lives. Julie was the kind of girl who attracts men without even trying.

COUNTRY DOCTOR
Paula Lindsay

When Evan Richmond bought a practice in a remote country village he did not realise that a casual encounter would lead to the loss of his heart.

ENCORE
Helga Moray

Craig and Janet realise that their true happiness lies with each other, but it is only under traumatic circumstances that they can be reunited.

NICOLETTE
Ivy Preston

When Grant Alston came back into her life, Nicolette was faced with a dilemma. Should she follow the path of duty or the path of love?

THE GOLDEN PUMA
Margaret Way

Catherine's time was spent looking after her father's Queensland farm. But what life was there without David, who wasn't interested in her?

HOSPITAL BY THE LAKE
Anne Durham

Nurse Marguerite Ingleby was always ready to become personally involved with her patients, to the despair of Brian Field, the Senior Surgical Registrar, who loved her.

VALLEY OF CONFLICT
David Farrell

Isolated in a hostel in the French Alps, Ann Russell sees her fiancé being seduced by a young girl. Then comes the avalanche that imperils their lives.

NURSE'S CHOICE
Peggy Gaddis

A proposal of marriage from the incredibly handsome and wealthy Reagan was enough to upset any girl — and Brooke Martin was no exception.

A DANGEROUS MAN
Anne Goring

Photographer Polly Burton was on safari in Mombasa when she met enigmatic Leon Hammond. But unpredictability was the name of the game where Leon was concerned.

PRECIOUS INHERITANCE
Joan Moules

Karen's new life working for an authoress took her from Sussex to a foreign airstrip and a kidnapping; to a real life adventure as gripping as any in the books she typed.

VISION OF LOVE
Grace Richmond

When Kathy takes over the rundown country kennels she finds Alec Stinton, a local vet, very helpful. But their friendship arouses bitter jealousy and a tragedy seems inevitable.

CRUSADING NURSE
Jane Converse

It was handsome Dr. Corbett who opened Nurse Susan Leighton's eyes and who set her off on a lonely crusade against some powerful enemies and a shattering struggle against the man she loved.

WILD ENCHANTMENT
Christina Green

Rowan's agreeable new boss had a dream of creating a famous perfume using her precious Silverstar, but Rowan's plans were very different.

DESERT ROMANCE
Irene Ord

Sally agrees to take her sister Pam's place as La Chartreuse the dancer, but she finds out there is more to it than dyeing her hair red and looking like her sister.